I0760823

BLOOD BROTHERS BEYOND

A Mortal Techniques story

Cover Art: Andrew Maleski

Cover Design: STK• Kreations

www.robjhayes.co.uk

A MORTAL TECHNIQUES NOVEL

BY

ROB J. HAYES

For Patrick

A NOTE FROM THE AUTHOR

Hi all!

Thanks for picking up Blood Brothers Beyond. I wanted to take this opportunity to say that the Mortal Techniques books are a series of standalone stories, set in an Asian-inspired sword & sorcery world. Each book can be read independently of the others.

They are my love letter to martial art films, anime, and eastern mythology.

Publication order is:

Never Die
Pawn's Gambit
Spirits of Vengeance
Century Blade (Short story)
Blood Brothers Beyond (Novella)

Thank you!

ROB

A family not founded, but forged in
fair fame.
With souls sparked from embers,
though crimson their name.

Their bonds are like iron, strong as
stone withstanding flood.
Nothing can stop them, nor break
apart the Brothers Blood.

Yet betrayal erodes the memory, foul
treachery from within.
The love they held for each other, grows
ethereal, wears thin.

And on the eve of forgetting, each and
every gone their way.

One last great adventure,
to my brothers
from beyond the grave.

THE BODY OF YOUNGEST BLOOD

From roads once travelled.
Drawing power from old earth.
Eyes to the mountain.

"Six Element Sword Style: Foundations of Earth."

Three men faced Ichiro. Three. Just three. Back in the day, the bounty would have attracted five times that and they'd still have expected to lose. But three? Three was an insult, was what it was.

The dusty road cleared of bystanders; merchants and farmers, and one pop-up wine stall vendor not wanting to get involved. Even the clouds high above seemed to pull back from the impending violence, and the blistering sun shone down on them all oppressively.

The three lawmen spread out, looking to surround Ichiro. He let them. The fundamental element to Foundations of Earth was to plant your feet and claim your space. He imagined a circle in the dirt around him, six feet across. That was his space, his territory, his world. And he pitied anyone who tried to invade it.

"Surrender, Blood Ichiro," said the lawman with a potato-shaped nose. "And no one needs to get hurt here." He carried a katana and was circling to get behind Ichiro.

Ichiro yawned dramatically. "The sword that rings loudest is the first to break." That definitely sounded like something a master of the blade would say.

"Huh?" said Potato Nose, now behind Ichiro.

Ichiro sighed. "Peace is the first resort for those unable to make war."

The lawman in front of him, a broad fellow with a bald head save for a scrappy, drooping fringe stopped his advance and frowned. "That's backwards."

"No it's not," Ichiro said.

"Is too," said The Fringe. "The Art of War wrote that *War is the first resort of those unwilling to consider peace.*"

Ichiro thought about it. It had been a long time since he'd studied philosophy, and that did have more of a ring to it.

"I'm right," said The Fringe.

"Bugger off!" said Ichiro.

"Last chance to surrender," said Potato Nose.

Bollocks to all the waiting around. Ichiro never did have the patience for foreplay. He swung his katana in a wide arc, dipping the blade so it trailed in the dirt.

"Bulwark," Ichiro whispered. His Foundations of Earth technique ripped a wall of crumbling dirt out of the ground in a half circle before him, cutting off The Fringe and his comrade with four chins. Potato Nose charged from behind, a battle cry snarling from his lips. He crossed into Ichiro's circle.

Ichiro turned on steady feet and met the stab, knocking it aside with a strength that flowed up from the earth and into his core. Potato Nose stumbled past him, unbalanced. Ichiro whipped his katana down and both flesh and bone parted before steel. One of Potato Nose's arms hit the dirt inside of Ichiro's circle. A second later, the man dropped to his knees and started screaming. It was a perfectly reasonable response, all things considered, but the wailing was a little distracting and Ichiro still had two men to fight, so he smacked Armless on the back of the head with his katana's tsuka, then kicked him out of the circle.

The Fringe shouldered through the crumbling bulwark and froze, staring at the dismembered arm. Four Chins rounded the earth wall, roared in anger, and leapt forward, over his fallen comrade and into Ichiro's circle. A second later, he fell out of it again, missing a leg below the knee.

The Fringe stared in horror at the body parts. Ichiro nudged a bloody hand with his boot. "I'm starting a collection. Care to donate?"

The Fringe shook his fringe. "Very wise," Ichiro said. He wiped down his blade, then re-sheathed it and walked past the last able-bodied lawman. "Even the tiger bows its head to the dragon." He was confident he got that quote right, at least.

There was a loud clapping from over by the pop-up wine stall. Ichiro scowled as he made his way over. Daijiro had arrived, and judging by the cart and donkey, he'd brought their charge with him. Daijiro had always been a big man, but in the years since Ichiro had seen him, he appeared to have gotten bigger, or possibly just a bit rounder. He still kept the sides of his head shaved and wore his long hair in a single braid, and his wide grin was as infectious as ever. He was wearing a patchwork of light furs in the Nash style, despite the heat of the day, and had the gall to not even look sweaty.

"I see you still like to make a dramatic show of things, Aniki," Daijiro said, sipping from a shallow wine cup.

"I see you still like to sit on the side-lines while I do all the work," Ichiro shot back.

"Well, you and Subaru were always so much quicker to start the fighting thing. I'm more of a negotiator," he said, placing a hand over his heart as if he hadn't just told the world's most blatant lie.

The wine vendor, one Tsin Xao if the sign above was to be believed, glanced at the spear Daijiro had leaned against his stall. There was a thick fur wrapping covering the blade, but the notched haft left no one in any doubt as to the action the weapon had seen.

"Some might say negotiator," Ichiro said. "I say you're a lazy freeloader."

Daijiro spread his hands and grinned. "It's good to see you, Aniki."

Ichiro stepped towards his oldest friend and they embraced. Daijiro clutched him tight and Ichiro slapped his back. "You, too, brother. You, too."

When they parted, Daijiro had a rueful expression on his face. "Shame about the circumstances though, eh?"

Ichiro glanced at the cart and frowned, then he turned his gaze to where the Heaven's Trail mountain dominated the horizon.

"I swore I'd never come back here," he said softly, glaring at the mountain range like he could scare it into scarpering off back over the horizon.

"True," Daijiro said. "But you also once swore you could eat an entire plate of bull testicles, then vomited all over Rock Jaw Jun."

Ichiro smiled at the memory. "Rock Jaw was so angry I thought he'd bite my nose off."

"He probably would have, but Subaru bought him a drink, then serenaded him like his long-lost love. How did those lyrics go?"

"I forget, thankfully."

Daijiro grinned. "My darling, my love, my bulging Hitotsume. I yearn to swell your girth and swallow your magnitude."

Ichiro couldn't help but laugh. "I'd never seen Rock Jaw so embarrassed."

"I think the old bastard was a little aroused, to be honest."

"Still," Ichiro said, frowning at the cart again. "I don't want to be here, brother."

Daijiro draped a thick arm over his shoulders and turned him towards the wine stall. "We'll get to that, Aniki. First things first. A drink. To the Brothers Blood, reunited one last time."

There was only one rickety stool in front of the wine stall, so Daijiro pushed it towards Ichiro, then sat on nothing, holding perfectly still as though the show off wasn't holding himself up by nothing but a ridiculous display of core strength.

"Welcome to Tsin Xao's House of Refreshment," said the oily wine vendor as he poured them each a cup of wine. "We serve only the finest Hosan wines."

"Hear that, brother," Ichiro said. "Only the finest Hosan swill. This is Ipia, don't you have anything with a bite to it?"

"Leave him be, Aniki," said Daijiro, smiling. "Let the poor fellow do his job."

Ichiro whisked up his cup, not caring that he spilled a few drops. "To brotherhood," he said a bit more bitterly than intended. Daijiro repeated the words, then they tapped their cups together and drank.

"Gah!" Ichiro almost spat the wine out. "Horse piss tastes better than this!"

"How would you know?" the vendor mumbled as he refilled their cups.

Daijiro barked out a laugh. "Actually, he does. There was this time—"

"No!" Ichiro snapped. Some memories he did not want to relive.

"To Subaru," Daijiro said, holding up his cup.

Ichiro knocked back his wine without repeating the toast.

"What's with the furs?" Ichiro asked as the cups were refilled.

Daijiro shrugged. "We have a mountain to climb. I have to look the part." He reached over and pinched Ichiro's sleeve. "I see you're still wearing this old thing."

Ichiro's haori had once been a deep black, but had long since faded to dark grey, the vibrant overlapping yellow triangles of the pattern now misshapen, fraying blobs of brown. The white crane emblem on the back was pristine though, mostly because he paid to have it re-sewn. He'd long since done away with the hakama, preferring a good sturdy pair of trousers instead. "It's my house haori," he said.

"Oh, I know," Daijiro said. "But your house disowned you two decades ago for... well, for all the banditry."

"Why do you think I still wear it?" he said with a grin.

"I'll drink to that. To family."

Ichiro tapped his cup. "To family." He drank and then turned his cup over to signal he wanted no more.

"Let's get on with it," he said as he slipped off the stool and strode to the cart.

It was a rickety old thing, little more than two wheels slapped to a few planks of wood, with a harness for the old donkey lethargically rooting in the dust for weeds. Ichiro edged past the donkey, which eyed him but said nothing, which he was thankful for because they weren't supposed to talk, but sometimes they did and then shit always went badly. There was a body lying in the cart, wrapped head to toe in white bandages, so not a bit of skin was showing. It smelled of herbs to stave off the stench of death and looked too small to contain an entire life. Especially one as big as Subaru's.

Ichiro heard footsteps as Daijiro stepped up beside him, head bowed. For a few seconds, they both stared down at their brother.

"You sure he's in there?" Ichiro said.

Daijiro huffed. "Pretty sure. I didn't exactly lift the bandages to take a peek. Wouldn't be respectful, you know?"

"It could be a trick. Knowing that arsehole, he's probably waiting up at the summit with a—"

"It's him, Aniki," said Daijiro mournfully. "That would be a step too far even for Subaru. He's gone."

Ichiro grunted but said nothing.

Daijiro put a hand on Ichiro's shoulder. "He arrived at my dojo two days ago, just like he is. The priest said they'd preserved him, as was his orders, and they gave me a letter he wrote. His last request." He reached into his furs and pulled out a wrinkled parchment. Ichiro took it and read.

GET ME INTO HEAVEN, BROTHER. I'M COUNTING ON YOU. AND TELL ANIKI HE HAS TO HELP.

Ichiro growled and scrunched up the note. It was just like Subaru. Always getting himself into trouble, then begging Ichiro and Daijiro to get him out of it. He'd been doing it all his life and now he was doing it one last time even in death. Ichiro tossed the screwed-up letter in the dirt and stalked to the front of the cart.

"Let's get this over with," he said and tugged the donkey into motion.

Daijiro paused and retrieved the note, taking a moment to smooth it out before pocketing it and hurrying to catch up.

The Oka mountain range stretched before them like a sullen boil on the horizon; oppressive, obnoxious, and foreboding. It was said, if a body was burned in the temple up on the summit of Koma mountain, at the height of the Heaven's Trail, their soul would go to heaven, no matter the things they had done in life. So, of course, Subaru wanted them to do it because there was certainly no other way he was getting in. No other way any of them were going to heaven. But there was a problem, something Subaru's note conveniently glossed over. The Heaven's Trail was guarded by vicious bandits, voracious heroes, and all manner of terrible yokai. They couldn't just climb their way to the top, they were going to have to fight their way up.

THE VILLAGE OF THE THOUSAND FALLS

Fleeting are echoes.
New truths bury older lies.
Hearts yet thunder on.

RINGEN VILLAGE HAD ALWAYS NESTLED SNUGLY AT THE base of the Thousand Falls that emptied from the Oka mountain range around it. Once, it had been a quaint little settlement of monks, filled with shrines to the various gods, living off the land, and paying tribute to heaven, earth, and the many, many, many hells. Last time Ichiro had been to Ringen was two decades ago, just weeks after being banished by his father. He'd come seeking guidance from the monks, but found something very different instead, and it had set his life on a dark path only the love of two brothers had pulled him away from.

It was fair to say Ringen had changed a lot in the last twenty years. For one, the monks were out. That's what happened when men and women dedicated to peace and worship came up against monsters who believed in nothing but violence and profit.

It being a well-known fact that having your body burned at the summit of Heaven's Trail got you past the Jade Gates no questions asked, meant that it was a popular spot for bereaved loved ones desperate to see their dearly departed all happy and eternal in the spirity realm of heaven. Or joining their ancestors in the stars above, or whatever people believed these days, it was all the same crap to Ichiro. So of course, bandits and merchants had moved in to charge the poor pilgrimaging bastards down to their under wrappings for the privilege. Add to that, the fact that everyone knew all sorts of god-touched ancient artefacts fell out of heaven and trickled down the mountain, and there was also a constant stream of treasure hunters showing up in Ringen for the chance to find some divine loot. No one liked to mention that all sorts of restless spirits also wandered out of heaven and found their way down the trail, because nothing scared off potential wealthy victims like stories of crazed yokai eating your eyeballs or following you around for the rest of your life and watching you pee.

So, it was with no surprise Ichiro found himself stopped before the bridge that crossed the mighty Tenkari river into Ringen. The Oka mountains loomed before them, massive and craggy, sometimes so festooned with clinging trees it was green as an emerald, other times coated so thickly in snow, it was pale as a whore's painted arse.

"Entry fee," said a snide bookish man as they approached the old toori gate that signalled the village outskirts. The 'tax men' had set up stakes around the toori to act as a makeshift wall, and there were three armed thugs lounging nearby, one of whom kept picking his nose and staring at whatever he found like it might actually be gold if he just squinted hard enough.

Daijiro ushered the donkey to a stop and folded his arms over his broad chest, grinning like Champa, the god of laughter. "This oughta be good. You deal with it, Aniki."

Ichiro was already stepping forward. He'd always been the one of the Brothers Blood who dealt with these matters because, as Subaru liked to say, Ichiro coming from a high-born family gave him a certain *Bugger off, you are beneath me* kind of presence that you just couldn't learn as a commoner.

"You a shintei?" asked the bookish man. He was unarmed, as opposed to his comrades, and wore a pair of spectacles that had no lenses to them.

Ichiro sighed. "Do I look like a shintei?"

The man looked him up and down. "That's why I'm asking."

"No." The shintei were a caste of warriors who had once been a dominant power in Ipia but had been all but wiped out by some catastrophe.

"Hmm," the man said and pushed the pointless spectacles further up his nose. "Entry is five lien each, three for the cart, and seven for the donkey."

Ichiro made a show of dropping one hand to his katana hilt. "Twenty lien is a lot just for entry. Why is the donkey seven?"

The tax man sniffed and wrinkled his nose. "Donkeys shit wherever they please. It needs cleaning up. Maintenance costs, you see."

Ichiro leaned to the side and glanced past the man. There was horse dung all over the bridge, and no one looked bothered about cleaning it.

"Twenty lien, hmm?" Ichiro said as he inspected the man. He was wearing a brown suit over a white shirt, a Cochtan fashion, and a purse hung from his leather belt. Ichiro smiled. "Okay."

He drew his katana in a fluid upward cut. The man screeched in panic. Ichiro slotted his katana back into its saya and leaned forward, catching the man's purse before it hit the floor. The man was still frozen in terror, probably wondering which body part was about to drop off. His armed friends were only now lumbering to their feet, but Daijiro stepped forward, thick arms crossed, and they clearly thought better than intervening.

"Twenty, was it?" Ichiro asked as he rifled through the purse. He counted twenty-five lien inside. He pulled out five lien, then tossed the purse back to the man. "There you go. Entry paid. Oh, and for the trouble." He flicked the man another lien, then pocketed the remaining four.

Through the toori, the great bridge stretched out before them. Despite the many pillars sunk deep into the rock, anchoring the bridge, Ichiro couldn't help but feel unsteady, as if the raging rapids below would tear the bridge, and them, away any moment. The noise of the water was deafening, and errant drops of spray cascaded over the lip of the bridge to pelt him in the face. From the bridge, Ichiro could see up into the winding valley between the mountains, and the thousand falls delivering so much water to the land far below. And there, sitting high above, at the top of an immense set of stone steps, sat a ten-level pagoda. Beyond that pagoda was where the Heaven's Trail started, threading upwards through the forest and into the mountain range before finally ending at the Koma mountain.

Ringen was a town built across many levels. Taking a lesson from the broad-leafed, stubborn trees that infested the place, the town clung to the rocks wherever it could, as the water from the Thousand Falls rushed and crashed around it, joining the Tenkari river in a furious tumult. In most towns, roads were dirt or stone, but in Ringen, they were wooden bridges, and curving sets of steps built into the rock itself. The donkey, or Lump as Daijiro insisted on calling the beast, struggled with its footing, but soldiered on regardless. Ichiro kept an eye on it, listening every time it huffed in case it started speaking.

There was plenty of foot traffic on the bridges. Some were couriers or artisans, others were vagrants or common folk just trying to go about their day. There were armed bandits everywhere, lounging on steps up to homes or in front of taverns, or posturing in small groups towards other thugs. It seemed there was more than one warlord ruling the bridges of Ringen these days. It almost made Ichiro feel at home. The Brothers Blood had never held control of a village or town, but the three of them had once been known and feared by bandits all across Ipia. They were the good old days.

On one level, the network of bridges collided into a wooden square where people crowded, and merchants hawked whatever shifty wares they could. Ichiro counted three brothels nearby, each one clinging to a different rocky outcropping. Painted whores lounged behind ripped and mouldering paper screens, calling obscene offers to everyone who went by. Ichiro chuckled at it all. The monks of old would have pitched a fit to see what their tranquil village had become. He laughed even harder when he saw a bald man in a monkish robe climbing the steps to a whore house, a few lien clutched in his hands. The sign outside the brothel read 'Madam Wang's Little Oyster'.

"Subaru would have loved this place," Daijiro shouted over the roaring falls and press of humanity.

Ichiro grunted as he shoved an old beggar out of the way. He was using his katana, still sheathed, to wave the milling crowd away from their path. Daijiro was right though, Subaru loved places like Ringen. The seedier the better, as far as their youngest brother was concerned.

"Do you remember that time in Kodachi? At The Plucked Quill," Daijiro said as he paced near the back of the cart. Ichiro remembered it well. The imperial capital was always memorable, especially when Madam Fuse Chitari was involved.

"We were supposed to be stealing the Star Emerald, but you bungled the snatch."

Ichiro gritted his teeth and seethed. He had not bungled the snatch at all. He'd been halfway through picking the lock on the vault door when Subaru heard a woman reciting poetry, which happened to be two things his arsehole younger brother could never resist. It turned out the woman in question was Empress Ryoko's favourite niece, and she apparently had a weakness for men of obvious low standing, questionable personal hygiene, and a vast repertoire of bawdy poems. Which would have been fine except her husband was none other than the legendary bounty hunter The Laws of Hope, AND he was bathing in the next room. Of course, Daijiro saw none of that because he was outside making sure none of the guards patrolled too close to the window; their only escape route.

"You two burst out of the mansion window like your arses were on fire," Daijiro continued. "It was all I could do to get my flower cart in front of the doorway to slow the soldiers down. You remember, Aniki? By the time I figured out you'd ducked into the Plucked Quill, they had half the city looking for you, and those descriptions were pretty spot on."

Feeling more than a little sour at Daijiro's butchered retelling, Ichiro snarled at a merchant offering sanctified spirit wards, and hauled on the donkey's mane to speed the beast through the square. The donkey snorted and sounded suspiciously like it was telling him to bugger off.

The truth about that old caper was that Ichiro himself had never been spotted, and the soldiers only had a description of Subaru, though that was detailed as it had come from the very same woman he had been halfway to undressing when he was caught. Despite that, Ichiro had stayed by his youngest brother's side even after hearing Madam Chitari's plan.

"They painted you up real nice, slipped a couple of melons down your dresses, and you and Subaru walked right out of the city with your pretty arses shaking. All while the very soldiers looking for you were busy drooling over your skirts."

That much, at least, was spot on.

"You made a very fetching woman, Aniki."

That was a step too far, and Ichiro rounded on Daijiro. "I made for a hideous woman, Daijiro. I looked like a bloody tengu in a dress. Subaru, on the other hand, somehow suited it like he was born to the paint and perfume." He fumed. "AND Chitari only gave *him* melons, made him look like the most well-stocked whore in all of Ipia. They stuck oranges down my dress. I had no cleavage at all, damn that woman!"

Daijiro was grinning as he sauntered along, leaning on the cart. "Do you want to know something Subaru said I was never to tell you?"

Ichiro sighed and led the donkey onto the next bridge leading up to the stone stairs. "No!"

"Bah!" Daijiro said, giving Subaru's corpse a little nudge. "He won't mind now, what with being dead and all."

"No!" Ichiro repeated. He had no wish to relive their glory days, nor gossip about his little brother's perversions. As far as he was concerned, this was just a job.

They walked in silence for a while and the squeak of the cart's wheels across the wet wooden bridges got on Ichiro's nerves. Or maybe it was that he was lying to both his brother and himself.

"Tell me," he mumbled.

Daijiro cleared his throat. "He got a bit of a liking for it after that caper. Subaru sometimes dressed up as a woman and went about town. Not to do anything. He said he just liked the way it felt. Liked the way people stared at him when they thought he was a woman."

Ichiro walked in silence for a while, keeping his hand on his katana hilt just because it felt comfortable. "He never told me he did that."

"I know," Daijiro said. "He said he didn't think you'd understand. The why of it, you know. Just dressed like that because he liked it."

"I would have understood," Ichiro said defensively. But he was already wondering if it was true. His little brother wearing a dress just because he enjoyed feeling like a woman. It made Ichiro uncomfortable. Not that it mattered now Subaru was gone, but it led to another, bigger question that did: What else did he not know about his little brother?

THE LAST MONK OF TRUE RESOLVE

Lessons like water.
Only in flow taking root.
Skips on calm surface.

"That's a lot of steps," Daijiro said, staring up into the crowded stone steps winding up through a snaking crevice in the rock. Water dripped down walls slick with spongy moss, and a light drizzle misted the air as though it were raining, but it was just spray from one of the Thousand Falls high above.

"You're the one insisting on this star-cursed pilgrimage," Ichiro said. He peered, squinting and had to admit that Daijiro was right, it was a lot of steps, and Ichiro was not looking forward to climbing them. But it was the only way to reach the start of the Heavenly Trail.

"So," Daijiro said, starting up the steps. "Should we give up here and leave our little brother to his tour of the many many hells?

We tried, Subaru. But, you know... it was a lot of steps, and my knees aren't what they used to be."

Ichiro drew in a deep breath and sighed it out so dramatically Daijiro had to have heard. "No, I suppose not." It was just like Subaru to tap out before any of the hard work needed doing. Besides, he supposed the donkey was going to be doing most of the effort.

Ichiro glared at the donkey. "I dare you to complain."

The donkey flicked its tail, twitched its ears, then set about hauling the cart up the steps. Ichiro walked behind it to give the cart a push whenever the wheels got caught.

Each step had a stone statue to one side of it. Some were small, nestled away in a corner, while others were large, dominating half the step. Many were eroded by time and weather, or defaced by disrespectful visitors. Once, a long time ago, the statues were maintained by the monks. Each one had a little wooden shrine before it, and incense was burned at those shrines daily. Visitors to Ringen, and the trail above, would leave donations at some of the shrines, offerings to whichever god or spirit they were dedicated to. It was a tradition that seemed to have lapsed.

Daijiro paused on every step, bowed his head to the statue, and whispered a quick prayer. He'd never been particularly religious before, none of the Brothers Blood had been, but they'd all seen enough over the years and their adventures to know it was always worth a kind word to appease the gods rather than risk angering them with a callous silence. Ichiro kept his peace though. Daijiro would have to be appeasing enough for the both of them.

The cart stuck, one wheel bumping against an uneven step. The donkey sighed and glanced back at Ichiro. He was sure it almost said something. Ichiro put his shoulder to the cart and heaved. It trundled up over the step. The donkey blew out its lips and it almost sounded like 'thanks'.

"I remember..." Ichiro said, heaving for air, "these steps... being easier."

Daijiro bowed his head to another statue. "That's right, you've been this way before. You were younger then, though, eh? Not as out of shape."

"Bastard!" Ichiro swore. "I'm not out of shape, I'm... just tired from a day's hard travel. I didn't do the trail last time though, just visited Ringen."

"Oh yeah," Daijiro said, shooting Ichiro an apologetic look. "This is where you met Sensue."

Ichiro nodded as he heaved the cart up another step. Sensue had been a brief light in his life when all else had seemed dark. He'd come to Ringen looking for guidance and instead had found her. They'd crossed blades and she'd stolen his heart. For five blissful, challenging days, they had been the entire world. Nothing but Sensue's lopsided little smile mattered a damn. They'd made love under the grandest of the Thousand Falls, and paid a monk to marry them before the eyes of the gods. Then it had all come crashing down. Ichiro had given his heart, his happiness, and his soul to a dying woman. Sensue hadn't come to Ringen to find herself, or seek guidance, she had come to make her way up Heaven's Trail and take her own life at the summit, forcing her way into heaven despite her chequered past.

He never even knew if she made it. She wouldn't let him go with her, wouldn't let him risk his own life for her afterlife. And he had let that argument sway him. He had been a coward and he had taken the easy way out rather than fighting for the woman he loved. He didn't know if Sensue was even now shining down on him from the stars, amidst her ancestors, or if the dangers of the trail had claimed her life and forced her to languish in the hells. He would never know. And no matter the decades that had passed, that unknowing ate at him like a tide chewing away at a cliff face.

The crevice walls seemed to close in on Ichiro as he brooded, slogging up the steps behind the cart carrying Subaru. Long ago, he had come to Ringen in a darkness of spirit he thought too bleak to bear. But in this village, he had found light, only to have it ripped away. And when he left Ringen, the darkness had been greater than any black could know. Not because he had lost the love of his life, he was happy just to have had those five days with her. But because he had failed her. Because he had let Sensue turn him away. He had let her attempt the trail alone. That had been the darkest time in his life, and it had taken meeting Daijiro and Subaru to make him see the light again.

Ichiro felt a big hand on his shoulder, pulling him out of his brooding reverie. Daijiro had dropped back to walk next to him. "You alright, Aniki?"

Ichiro glanced at his younger brother, then at their fool of a youngest brother in his funeral shawl. He put his shoulder to the cart and pushed again. "I'm fine," he growled. "Let's just get this over with."

By the time they reached the top of the steps, Ichiro was sweaty and simmering in a foul temper. He wasn't even certain where the dark mood had come from; he had dealt with the loss of Sensue long ago. The donkey let out a grateful huff that sounded suspiciously like 'finally' and then gave Ichiro a side-eyed stare. He slapped the possibly normal beast on the flanks and it trundled on, pulling the cart along a worn dirt path that snaked between cramped buildings with a close forest of auburn leafed canopy overhead. A few curious faces stared out of windows above, but they vanished whenever Ichiro looked at them.

"Do these folk seem nervous to you?" Daijiro asked as he dropped back.

Ichiro nodded slowly. "Yeah. Do you hear that?" There was a regular percussive thumping from somewhere ahead of them, each thump accompanied by shouts.

Daijiro chuckled. "Reminds me of that time we broke into the Lotus Maiden's vault."

"You're still laughing at the name?"

"Of course I'm still laughing at the bloody name. I mean, she called herself the Lotus Maiden, and built herself a vault below her mansion. Can't tell me she didn't know what she was doing. But you remember the traps?"

"I do."

"And the ceiling?"

Ichiro sighed. "In crushing detail."

"Nice one! Every time it dropped a foot, there was that thump."

Ichiro dropped his hand to his katana, resting it there. "I remember. Have you ever wondered why her crushing ceiling trap took so long to... well, crush? Why it dropped foot by foot rather than squash us in an instant?"

"To give us time to escape, of course," Daijiro said happily. "Which we did."

"And to give the Lotus Maiden time to get into position."

"Which she was."

"So she could kick our arses."

"Which she definitely did," Daijiro said. "Oh, I see where you're going, Aniki. You think you're very smart and that you were the only one to figure out the whole thing was a job interview."

Ichiro shut his mouth. That was exactly what he had thought. The Lotus Maiden had hired them through a third party, pitted them against her traps, then tested their skills. And just when all three Brothers Blood realised how outmatched they were, she offered them a job, because it turned out the beautiful and seemingly innocent Lotus Maiden was actually the boss of a powerful and extensive crime syndicate. And from that moment on, the Brothers Blood worked for her. Because the alternative was death. Probably quite a gruesome one, considering the bitch's reputation, and Ichiro for one had no desire to feel his balls pulled out through his nostrils.

The cramped buildings ended, and the forest peeled away to reveal a rocky clearing on the edge of a cliff side overlooking Ringen below. The ten-storey pagoda that marked the beginning of the Heavenly Trail nestled on the edge of the cliff side. Gushing water from one of the Thousand Falls high above crashed down, barely missing the arched roofs before careening over the cliff, and droplets of water sparkled in the daylight, casting rainbows all over the clearing like some sort of wonder from the spirit realm.

Another thump, followed by shouting drew Ichiro's attention to the pagoda. There were five swarthy bandits crowding the doorway, using a stripped log as a battering ram. Judging by the dents, scrapes, and splinters they were making a piss-poor job of it but carving out some headway regardless. It wouldn't be long before they caved the door in, for whatever nefarious purpose they were up to.

"We should go check that out," said Daijiro.

"Not our problem, or our purpose," Ichiro said. "The trail is that way." He pointed to where the dirt path bent away from the pagoda back towards the forest and a gloomy path through it marked by a bright red and gold painted toori.

Daijiro tucked his hands into the front of his furs and kept walking. "But isn't it customary to give the monks a donation before starting on the trail?"

Ichiro sighed and glanced at the donkey. It gave him a long-suffering stare but said nothing. Then they both set off after Daijiro.

"Is there a party in there you fine folks weren't invited to?" Daijiro said cheerily as he approached. Ichiro followed a few steps behind.

The biggest of the bandits, a towering slab of a woman who

looked like she'd never met a door she hadn't head-butted her way through, turned and gave Daijiro a squinty stare.

"Who'er you?" she demanded, making it a threat by cracking scarred knuckles.

"We're just heading up the trail," Ichiro said. Daijiro nodded amiably. "Thought we'd see what the noise was about."

"Monks ain't paid their rent," said Big Ugly. "Boss wants them evicted."

"May the gods bless you with taste buds in every orifice!" A slurred shout bellowed from the other side of the door.

Big Ugly turned back to the door with a shout of her own. "Open up or when I get in there, I'll strip you naked and toss you over the falls!"

A muted mad giggle was followed by: "May the kami of the mountain turn all your bread to stone in your mouth so your teeth snap and you choke on your own blood... Bless you."

Big Ugly bellowed in rage, snatched up the log battering ram and slammed into the door on her own to prove she was stronger than the average oni.

Ichiro found his brother looking at him expectantly. He aimed a shrug back at Daijiro. "Not our problem," he said. Then turned back to the path and started walking.

After a few moments, Daijiro sighed and caught up, leaving the monk and the bandits to whatever fate would bring them. "What was it Subaru always used to say?" Daijiro asked as they paced towards the toori at the forest edge.

"Never dip your brush in another man's ink," Ichiro said.

Daijiro laughed. "Unless the paper is very fine. He never could follow his own advice. But not that. What was it?"

They walked in silence for a few seconds, listening to the distant thump. "She really would be better off with an axe," Ichiro said.

Daijiro clicked his fingers. "Got it. It was from that poem he used to quote."

"He used to butcher," Ichiro corrected.

Daijiro cleared his throat, also determined to butcher the poem.

> "Some men fight for money, a lavish
> reward. While others fight for love, and
> some for their lord.
> "But the spirit of banditry is not about
> gain. The truest of bandits fight for
> freedom, not fame.
> "I stand for the broken, the downtrodden,
> the oppressed. My blade cuts authority,
> pierces corruption through the chest.
> "When all is said and done, my rakish
> corpse laid to rest, I hope they will say I
> put kings, queens, and tyrants to the
> test."

Ichiro slowed to a halt. Subaru had loved that damned poem. It encapsulated the core of what had kept the Brothers Blood together for so long, and what had made them so feared and so hunted. Never take from the vulnerable or the needy, never strike those who could not strike back. Steal from the powerful, spend that money with the poor. Disrupt the systems of power and control.

Daijiro was looking at him, a knowing yet apologetic smile on his lips.

Ichiro sighed, thumbed his katana out of its saya, and started back towards the pagoda. "Six Element Style," Ichiro shouted as he bounded up the steps to reach the bandits. "Flow of Water."

The bandits turned to meet him, scrabbling for their weapons.

The first of them was in two pieces before they realised they were dead.

Ichiro sprang into the centre of the four remaining bandits and ducked under a sword swing, bringing his katana up in a two-handed slice. Another bandit fell in a spray of blood.

Just three remained; Big Ugly and her log, a pot-bellied fool with a rusty mace, and a rancid-looking man whose face was constantly twitching in either pain, rage, or possibly the desperate need to shit. But this was where Flow of Water was strongest, when he was outnumbered and surrounded. The sword style was all about fluid movements and broad, powerful strikes that washed opponents away one by one.

Ichiro flowed into another slice and Needs to Shit fell, wondering where his legs had gone. Pot Belly screamed and swung for Ichiro, but he slipped aside on nimble feet, knocked the attack away, then drove his sword up through Pot Belly's pot belly. And that left only...

Big Ugly's log slammed into Ichiro's chest and sent him flying back down the steps. He crashed into the dirt and groaned from the pain, which his body quickly gave up trying to catalogue and decided on *maybe just everywhere*.

Ichiro staggered back to his feet, using his katana as a crutch even as Big Ugly stamped down the stairs, waving her log about like a child with a favourite stick.

"How fucking dare you!" she snarled. "I am going to mount you on my log and use your face to break down the door." She paused and glanced at Daijiro.

He was leaning against the cart, his hands tucked into the front of his furs. "Oh, don't mind me. Get to the mounting, it sounds interesting."

Big Ugly grunted and jumped down the last two steps, her feet squelching in the muddy ground.

The Flow of Water stance wasn't suited to fighting single,

powerful opponents, but Ichiro decided he couldn't be bothered switching styles.

"Crashing Waves," he said and chopped his sword downwards through the air.

Big Ugly sneered. "What—"

A torrent of water slammed into her from above, driving her to one knee. Ichiro slashed to the side and another spout of water gushed into her from behind, making her stumble. He sliced upwards and a geyser shot from beneath her feet, dazing her. Ichiro ran two steps and leapt, spinning in mid-air and slashing his katana.

He landed on sodden ground and slipped his katana back into its saya. Big Ugly's head thumped to the earth, followed a moment later by her giant body. All five bandits were dead.

Ichiro glanced over his shoulder at Daijiro. "You could have helped."

Daijiro shook his head as he dodged around bodies. "You looked like you had it." He stepped up to the door and knocked politely.

"Izumi, goddess of fog bless you with hair on your eyeballs!" slurred the voice from the other side of the door.

"That sounds unpleasant," Daijiro said, then cleared his throat. "Your assailants have all been vanquished."

A moments silence. Ichiro saw a face at a window above, there for a moment, then gone.

"How do I know it's not a trick?"

"A trick?" Daijiro asked. He nudged a torso with his foot. "This chap is in two pieces."

Ichiro laughed. "Remember Kongman the Ghost Hand?"

"Remember him?" Daijiro shivered. "A man oughta die when you chop that many things off him."

The splintered door burst open and a monk with a bulbous, veiny nose spilled out and into Daijiro's arms.

"Bless you. Bless you, great travellers. You've saved us all from a fate worse than death. A thousand blessings on you from the Lord of Heaven."

"Uh huh," Daijiro said. "Hope none of those come with warts on my cock or the like. Here, have you been drinking?"

"I can smell him from here," Ichiro said. He smelled like he'd been bathing in sake.

"Of course," slurred the monk as he pulled back from Daijiro. "It is Banjanat, the God of Drinking's ascension day. It is only right to pay tribute." He reached into his robes and pulled out a gourd, then took a swig and waved it at Daijiro. "A blessing?"

"No," Ichiro said.

"Maybe just one," Daijiro said and took a swig from the gourd, then broke into a coughing fit. He doubled over, waving the gourd at Ichiro.

Ichiro took the gourd, more curious than anything, and sniffed. The stench hit him like a slap from a trout. "Why does it smell like mouldy goat?"

The monk shrugged. "Ish made from goat's milk."

"How?" asked Daijiro.

"Why?" asked Ichiro. He drew in a deep breath, then swigged the foul stuff. If the smell was like being slapped by a fish, the taste was more like an ox stampede to the crotch. He doubled over, fighting the urge to vomit. The monk plucked the gourd from his limp fingers and swallowed down another mouthful with a grateful smacking of the lips.

"Will you be alright to get rid of the bodies?" Daijiro asked the drunken monk.

"This is Ringen," the monk said with a chuckle. "Bodies go missing all the time. I wouldn't worry about it."

Ichiro didn't fancy digging too far into that statement. "They won't send more after you?"

The monk giggled. "Oh, they always send more. We're the last monks in Ringen. We've gotten pretty good at resisting."

"Right," Daijiro said. "Well, we're looking for a blessing."

The monk waved the gourd his way again, but Daijiro shook his head. "Not that type. We're headed up the mountain to send our brother to heaven." He thumbed over his shoulder towards the cart. The donkey looked up, as if it had just been caught with its hand on another man's sword.

"Oh," the monk said sombrely. "Good luck. May the Gods watch over your journey, and may the mountain guide your feet. For what it's worth."

"What's that mean?" Daijiro asked.

The monk took another swig. "No one has made it up the trail in years. It's infested with dangers, and there's not enough of us left to secure it."

Daijiro glanced at Ichiro, frowning. "Well, we have to try. Thanks for the blessing, old man."

Ichiro wasn't so sure about that. He still thought the entire affair was a waste of time. Subaru was dead, and Ichiro didn't truly believe some inane ritual would lift his spirit out of hell, nor that his youngest brother deserved it anyway. He was there for Daijiro, though, and Daijiro believed it. He needed it. So Ichiro would get them all to the top of the mountain no matter what it took.

Ichiro nodded. "We have to try. Here..." He pulled four lien from his purse and handed them to the monk. "A donation from some bandits. Maybe use it to buy some real booze."

The monk giggled. "The gods provide all we need." He took the coins anyway.

Ichiro and Daijiro rejoined the path and started towards the forest edge and the start of Heaven's Trail. There was still a long way to go and a lot of mountain to climb.

THE FAVOUR OF THE FOX

Too good to be true.
Favour asked for no return.
Too true to be good.

When they reached the toori at the forest edge that marked the start of the trail, they found a bright orange fox sitting on the golden arch. Both the red and gold paint was long since flaking and fading away, and it only made the fox seem more vibrant. The beast's tail was long and tipped with black fur and it draped down, flicking back and forth. The fox watched them through eyes darker than tar.

"Will you look at that," Daijiro said, shaking his head. "It doesn't fear us at all. Don't you know, foxy, we could be viciously dangerous bandits." He chuckled at his jest and walked through the arch, leading the donkey and cart.

Ichiro stopped before the toori and met the fox's cool stare. He felt like the whole world was contained in that gaze; the four empires, the vast seas, the wild lands beyond, even the heavens and the stars themselves. At the same time, he also felt like its gaze was empty as the lifeless dead.

"You coming, Aniki?" Daijiro shouted. He and the donkey were a good ways up the path already into the forest. Ichiro wondered how long he'd been staring at the fox.

He shook the idle thoughts from his head, clapped his hands together, and bowed in a show of respect. The fox swished its tail. Ichiro hurried through the toori and caught up to Daijiro.

Contrary to the monk's dire warnings, the forest seemed a peaceful place. The trees were old and thick and gnarly, the leaves were a vibrant melange of reds and greens, the earth spongy underfoot, though the odd root broke through the soil to trip unwary hikers. Even the roar of the nearby falls was muted, and Ichiro heard birds calling to each other in an eternal patter of sing-song notes. Here and there, light shone through the canopy like white spears thrust down from heaven.

The path they followed was a winding one, ever sloping upwards, sometimes gently, other times so steep one of them had to walk behind the cart to make certain Subaru's corpse didn't slip off the back. Waystones marked the road every hundred paces or so, each one a squat, chubby little thing that made Ichiro think of a pudgy man, naked and leering, jealously hunched over a candle. And each of the way stones held a small red candle, the flame low and steady. It made Ichiro wonder who was maintaining the path and changing the candles, if the monks no longer left their last refuge of the pagoda.

"I see you're still telegraphing your technique," Daijiro said from his spot walking next to the donkey. "That old *Six Element style* thing."

"It's about honour," Ichiro said. "When you use a technique as powerful as the Six Element style, it's only honourable to let your opponent know it's coming."

"That's your father talking."

Ichiro sighed. "Some lessons are hard to unlearn." The truth was, he also wasn't sure his father was wrong about it. For all their differences, and they were myriad, they had always agreed on the correct use of the family's bloodline technique. But they had never agreed on what it should be used for. His father had always used his technique to uphold the regimes of the Ipian Empire and protect the ruling Ito family. Ichiro wanted to see it all come crashing down. It was a somewhat untenable difference in opinion, and the last thing his father had ever said to Ichiro was to call him an anarchist and a disgrace. He'd offered Ichiro the choice between an honourable death or banishment and dishonour. Death had never appealed to Ichiro.

"How is the old man?" Daijiro asked.

"Still alive."

Daijiro harrumphed. "Unlucky for us all, I say."

The cart bounced over a looping root, jostling Subaru's body. The donkey grumbled something that might have been 'bloody trees' or maybe just a disgruntled snort, and continued plodding on. The damage was done and the cart wheel had a pronounced wobble.

"You could have picked a sturdier cart. This piece of crap is one ill-placed pebble away from kindling."

Daijiro leaned over and glanced at the wobbling wheel. "I didn't pick anything. Cart and donkey came with the body. I figured Subaru organised it all before he dropped. Picking a shifty cart was probably one last prank. You know how he loved to joke around."

"This whole thing is a prank," Ichiro said bitterly. The donkey huffed as if agreeing.

Something was needling at him, like a stone in his shoe he just kept stepping on. "How did he die? If he had time to send you a note, to make arrangements for... for his body. What, or who, killed him?"

Daijiro shrugged and tucked his hands into the front of his furs. "Does it matter?"

"Of course it matters."

"Why?"

Ichiro gritted his teeth and walked around the cart to the front. He saw a flash of colour slipping through the trees, a ruddy blur. "What if someone killed him? He'll need avenging!"

"You think he'd want that?" Daijiro asked. "Some lawman or old nemesis, maybe a pissed off ex-lover finally catches up to him, and is good enough to do him in, you think Subaru would be angry?"

Ichiro had to admit it was unlikely. If someone was good enough or lucky enough to have got the better of Subaru, his note would be more likely to tell them to buy the killer a drink rather than point a finger and say 'get the bastard'. And the note hadn't said either, just asked them to make sure he went to heaven rather than sampling the delights of the hells.

"It just..." Ichiro sighed. "It doesn't seem right that there's no one to blame." He looked up to find Daijiro giving him a sympathetic look.

"Shut up!" Ichiro growled.

"I didn't say anything."

"You gave me that look."

Daijiro shook his head. "I gave you *a* look."

"It was *the* look. The *maybe there's no one to blame but ourselves* look."

"That sounds like a very complex look."

They walked in silence for a while. It was peaceful, comfortable, but then time spent with his brothers had always been that.

Ichiro always found he was most able to be himself with those who placed no expectations on him. His brothers had always been that; love and support, no matter what.

He spotted the flash of colour again, slinking through the trees, keeping pace with them.

"I think that fox is following us," Daijiro said, staring after the orange blur.

Ichiro squinted into the trees. "I'm not so sure it was a fox. There's more than just beast and man between heaven and us."

Daijiro chuckled. "Well, at least we're on the right path... Shiiii-it!" He pushed the donkey to a stop and glanced frantically up and down the path. "Where are the waystones?"

Behind and before them, the path was clear, not a waystone in sight. Ichiro couldn't say when he'd seen the last one, they'd definitely been following them at some point, but now they weren't.

"We could turn around, double back until we find them again."

Daijiro frowned as he peered down the path ahead. "Wait. I think there's a clearing ahead. We'll get our bearings and strike out from there." He slapped the donkey's arse to get it moving again.

A rustle to the left and another flash of orange that looked a lot like the fox, had Ichiro less than sure about the decision. He was certain he heard a soft tinkling laughter echoing through the trees, but if there was a woman nearby, he saw no sign.

The clearing was a small lake in the forest where trees crowded the shore, leaning over the crystal-clear waters, and the sun shone down through the gap in the canopy, glinting off the lapping waves. One of the Thousand Falls emptied high above and the water splashed down into the lake on the far side. There was a small island in the centre of the lake, with a lonely stone shrine atop a few steps, and a gentle wisp of smoke from burning incense sticks wafted up from the shrine. An old wooden bridge, festooned with frogs croaking in symphony led from the shore to the island. It was the most tranquil place Ichiro had ever seen. He sensed veiled danger.

"Well, isn't this something," Daijiro said.

"Something," Ichiro agreed.

"I'm gonna go pray for guidance," Daijiro said, already making for the frog-infested bridge. "If anyone can put us back on the right path, it's the Goddess Natsuko!"

Ichiro didn't disagree with his brother, but he had a feeling it would be in vain. He doubted any of the gods could hear them in the glade.

As Daijiro hopped along the bridge dodging warty little mines that seemed determined to leap under his feet, Ichiro paced along the shore, peering into the trees and hoping to spot a waystone. He thought it was pointless, but he hated sitting and doing nothing while they were lost.

Another tinkling laugh sounded behind him, and Ichiro turned to find the fox from the toori sitting there between him and the cart. Its bushy tail thumped the mossy ground once, then curled around its legs. It didn't seem hostile, but then neither did an arrow until someone loosed one at your face.

"Is this your forest?" Ichiro asked as he edged closer.

The fox tilted its head and watched him, but it didn't bolt.

"I know we're loud, and probably smelly, too. But we don't mean to disturb you. We're just passing through."

The fox blinked and looked out to the island where Daijiro had finished crossing and was kneeling before the shrine. The fox's tail thumped again and it seemed to be annoyed.

"He's praying to the wrong thing, isn't he?" Ichiro said, creeping closer still. "Natsuko has no sway here."

The tail thumped.

"None of the gods have influence here," Ichiro corrected. "This is your forest, your shrine." He took one last step, close enough to strike the fox. Then he knelt before it and bowed his head. "And we entered without paying tribute."

The fox blinked.

Ichiro reached into his haori and pulled out a leather pouch. "I don't have much, and even less I can afford to part with, but how about we share a meal?"

He pulled a strip of dried fish from the pouch, bit it and then laid the more generous half before the fox. The fox lowered its head, sniffed, then snatched up the dried fish. Only then did Ichiro eat his half. A meal shared was both a blessing and a tribute.

The fox's tail thumped, and it stared dark eyes at the shrine where Daijiro had finished praying to Natsuko and was lighting another incense stick. Judging by the fox's reaction, he had not given thanks to the spirits of the forest.

The tail thumped once more.

Just as Daijiro reached the bridge to cross back to shore, the water around him erupted as a toad the size of a small house exploded out of the water and slammed onto the little island.

"Shit!" Daijiro shouted as he ran across the bridge. He made it four steps before the great toads' mouth opened wide and a slimy pink tongue shot out like a shooting star and wrapped around his ankle. He pitched forward and hit the wooden bridge face first. The nearby frogs leapt on him, bouncing up and down on his back and head.

Ichiro shot to his feet, his katana already halfway out of its saya. He'd never fought a giant toad before, but he'd long believed just about anything died if you stabbed it enough. The toad was hauling Daijiro backwards towards its gaping mouth even as his hands clawed against the wood of the bridge.

It was no coincidence they ended up at the lake, nor was the toad that leapt out of the water only after Daijiro had finished his prayer. After he had unwittingly snubbed a spirit who held more power in the forest than even a god.

Ichiro slammed his katana back into its saya. The toad had Daijiro up to his waist in its mouth now. Ichiro turned and knelt before the fox, placing his forehead to the mossy ground.

"Great kitsune of the forest, forgive us both. We did not mean to trespass without your blessing, nor fail to offer tribute."

Daijiro gave a shout of panic, cut off as he disappeared into the toad's mouth, which snapped shut. Then the giant beast leapt into the water with a great splash, disappearing beneath the waves.

Ichiro turned back to find the fox staring at him, cold black eyes uncaring. "I offer to share my meal, it is all that I have. And... I, uh, offer a favour, freely given without constraint or reserve. Please, allow us to pass through your forest."

The clearing fell silent but for the gentle lapping of water against the shore and the croak of frogs on the bridge. The fox bowed its head and snapped up another bite of dried fish.

Daijiro burst out of the water like a stone from a sling, sailed past the bridge, and landed on the shore with a thump, all while choking and sputtering.

Ichiro bowed his head to the fox again. "Thank you!" He snapped a strip of dried fish in half and laid one side in front of the fox and tossed the other to Daijiro even as he rolled to his hands and knees. "Eat that!"

Daijiro was dazed, confused, and soaked to the bone. "Wha..."

"Just eat it!"

Daijiro sniffed. "I hate fish." Ichiro shot him a dangerous look until he popped it in his mouth and chewed. "Ugh! Tastes like salty arse."

The fox stood and swished its tail, then turned and strode past the donkey. The donkey did not hesitate to follow.

"What just happened?" Daijiro said. "Did I just get eaten by a giant frog?"

Ichiro shrugged and started after the fox and donkey. "It was a toad."

"You could have helped."

"You looked like you had it under control."

"Heh! I am soaked, and very confused. And are we following the fox now?"

Ichiro took one last look back at the lake, now tranquil once more. "It's no fox, brother."

THE GRAVEYARD OF FAILED DESTINIES

What death may reveal.
No end but oblivion.
In hearts of lovers.

THE DEFINITELY-NOT-A-FOX LED THEM THROUGH THE forest and sat by the last tree as Ichiro, Daijiro, donkey and cart moved past towards the rocky mountain trail.

Ichiro turned back once he was clear of trees, expecting to find the fox gone, but it sat there still, head tilted, dark eyes watching him. A not-so-subtle reminder of what their passage through the forest had cost them. A favour he could not refuse. Be it tomorrow, or ten years, or two lifetimes from now, one day the kitsune would come calling, and whatever it wanted, it would have. Not idly were deals with spirits made, and the stories all agreed that mortals rarely came out with the better end.

Ichiro turned from the forest and found the donkey staring at him. It snorted, and sounded a lot like it was saying 'fool', though

Ichiro had to admit that was probably a stretch. But the donkey had heard his offer to the kitsune, which was fine as long as the beast kept its peace. Daijiro didn't need to know what price Ichiro had paid for their passage. He didn't need the guilt.

The mountain path was strewn with rocks and boulders, but it was wide enough they could steer the wobbly cart around the worst of the rubble. To their right, the ground was mostly flat until it reached a sheer rise. To their left, the cliff side gave way sharply and they could peer down to the lush valley below. They'd already come a long way from Ringen, and its lights were nothing but a hazy glow far below, its noise lost in the whistling wind and roaring waterfalls.

"How much farther, do you think?" Daijiro asked.

Ichiro pointed towards a distant mountain, whose peak vanished into thick white clouds.

Daijiro blew out a long breath. "Far, then."

"Far and then a helping of all the way over there," Ichiro agreed. From what he knew, there were a few more mountain passes to cross yet, then Lord Manamanto's Gap, and the old fort that bridged it, and then they would reach the Koma mountain which they would still need to climb to reach the summit. Most people never finished the pilgrimage of Heaven's Trail. Most were smart enough not to bother trying.

"Guess we've been apart for a good long while, now I think on it. When did you learn all about spirits, then?" Daijiro asked as they hiked.

"I, uh, had cause to read a few old scrolls and tomes. Since we all went our separate ways, I've had more time to read."

"But less chance to fight."

Ichiro shot him a glare, but Daijiro shrugged. "Those books and scrolls told you the fox was, uh, what was it? A kitsune?"

"It was kind of a guess," Ichiro admitted. "There're many types of spirit that can posses an animal. Mononokes, shikigami. Even the restless spirits of the dead. But that fox had an old, powerful feel to it. I guessed it was a kitsune. They often take the guise of a fox."

"Huh. And the big frog?"

"It was a toad." Ichiro waggled his fingers. "Spirity stuff, I guess. An ogama, maybe. I'm no expert. When did you start worshipping the gods?"

"Who says I do?"

"Brother, you stopped at every shrine on the steps to offer a prayer. You all but insisted we help the monks. And when we were lost, the first thing you did was ask the gods for guidance."

Daijiro kicked a little pebble over the side of the cliff. "A man has to have something to hold on to. I was lost for a while after we all split up. I got myself into some trouble. A lot of trouble. Big trouble."

"Why didn't you come to me?" Ichiro asked.

Daijiro let out a loud snort. "And how would I have done that, Aniki? You were gone. You burnt every bridge when you left, told no one where to find you. Just vanished overnight without even a note to say why."

"I..." Ichiro trailed off before even starting. He had no excuse, at least not one Daijiro wanted to hear. He glanced back at the body in the cart. No excuse *he* wanted Daijiro to hear. "It was the only way to get free of her."

"Hmph, sure. Subaru refused to even say your name," Daijiro continued. "Just went on like nothing had changed, like you'd never even existed. Only he got all broody and sulky like he was making up for you not being there."

"I don't sulk. I'm just introspective."

"You weren't there, Ichiro. You were gone. So, when I said I was going to find you, Subaru spat like a viper and agreed I should go, but not come back! Him and his damned pride."

Daijiro slumped, belly sagging, as he let go of himself, too tired to hold it in any more. He stumbled over to a nearby boulder and sat, head bowed. The donkey, probably thinking it was time for a break and a snack, clapped over and poked Daijiro with its nose. He swatted the beast away. "You left us, Ichiro. And then I... I left him. All alone. And now he's gone."

Ichiro leaned against the cart, silent. He loved his brother, but he couldn't tell him the truth. Especially not now Subaru was gone. He wouldn't sully Daijiro's memory of their little brother like that. "What happened to you, Daijiro?"

Daijiro heaved a great sigh and sat a little straighter. "You broke our brotherhood, that's what. And I never even knew why. Bah! That's not fair of me. You made a choice, and wrong or not, it was your choice to make. But... You could have told me.

"I went looking for you. No idea what had happened and I thought... I thought you might need help. But our old life caught up with me. Lawmen snatched me just outside of Pyoto. They put me in the fighting pits, which I don't mind telling you are not a lot of fun."

He glanced down at his hands and Ichiro saw scars on his brother's knuckles he didn't recognise. "I beat my way through dozens of men," he said distantly. "Lost a few fights, too, though not many, I guess. Some matches... Some matches they didn't let you out of the pit until one of you stops breathing. And they watch you, see who you talk to in the cells. Anyone you make friends with... that's your next match. I did... things. I..." Daijiro trailed off, then took a great shuddering breath and skipped ahead, unwilling to share his guilt.

"Luckily, some monks from Henna Temple saw me fight and they were looking for someone to train the youngsters. They bought me, cleaned me up, fed me. They gave me a home in return for teaching them how to defend themselves against bandits." He chuckled suddenly. "I mean, irony like that, how can you not believe the gods are involved? The monks claimed the gods led them to me, and they pulled me out of something that felt a lot like one of the hells, so yeah... yeah, I started praying. And I find a peace in it I've never known before."

Daijiro all but leapt up, beaming and holding himself tight again like he hadn't just been broken. "Not the cheeriest of tales, but a happy ending. Well, maybe not for Subaru, but..." He leaned over the cart and patted the corpse on the shoulder. "Sorry for leaving, little brother. Right! Onwards." He slapped the donkey's flanks to get it moving again. It was a thin veneer of cheerfulness his brother wore, and Ichiro wondered how long until it cracked again.

"Daijiro. When I left, I didn't mean for you to... I'm sorry."

Daijiro shook his head a little wildly. "None of that, Aniki. Just... let's move on. Please."

It was strange that all three of them had once been so close, bonded far stronger than any blood ties. They had been together for over a decade, and now apart for only a handful of years. And yet, they had all changed so much in that time. There was so much he and Daijiro didn't know about each other now, and more they would never get to know about Subaru. Despite that, spending this time with his brothers, even with Subaru dead, felt like coming home after weeks on the road. Ichiro had missed them both so much.

"You really teach baby monks to fight now?" Ichiro asked as they approached a wooden bridge staked to the rock. It forded a rushing river that burst out, falling over the cliff side.

"Not just monks," Daijiro said. "It was at first, but they gave me a dojo and it seemed wasteful not to open it to anyone who wants to learn. I have a hundred students and ten disciples these days, all teaching *Quivering Palm* style martial arts!"

Ichiro raised an eyebrow. "Quivering Palm style?"

Daijiro laughed. "No idea, Aniki. When they pulled me out of the pits, they asked me what style I practiced. I said the first damned thing that came to mind. I'd have called it Blue Bollock style as long as they got me out of there."

"Blue Bollock style might be more fitting for a bunch of monks."

"Maybe. Maybe. But there was no way I was following those teachings." The bridge creaked underfoot and spray from the water slapped at them.

"So, what are you up to these days," Daijiro asked. "I found out you were in Nadama, but nothing else. What's the great Blood Ichiro doing with his life?"

Ichiro cleared his throat and stared into the spray. "I tch cigrafy kids," he mumbled.

The donkey snorted.

Daijiro narrowed his eyes. "What was that?"

Ichiro winced. "I teach calligraphy to children."

Daijiro paused, mouth open. He glanced at the donkey who flicked its ears. "You, the infamous Blood Ichiro, wielder of the Six Element style, victor of seventeen duels in the Salt Sovereign's Gauntlet, famed rebel against authority and familial power... Teach brush waving to noble shits?"

Ichiro opened his mouth to argue, then sighed. "Yes."

"Oh, how the mighty have fallen. Do you have a school, too?"

Another sigh. "Yes."

"Do they have to call you Sensei?"

He would never live this one down. "Yes."

By the time night fell, they had wound all the way around one mountain and crossed to another. It was a respectful distance travelled for one day and in the distance, Ichiro could just about make out Lord Manamanto's gap and see the looping arches of the great stone bridge that crossed it.

In the gathering gloom, they steered the cart off the trail and up a steep slope to a rocky plateau. A few stubborn trees clung to rocks here and there, their bark bone white, branches skeletal, and leaves blood red. Dotted all over the plateau were little piles of stones, hundreds of them all unmarked.

"What is this place?" Daijiro asked as he unhitched the donkey from the cart. It gave a grateful snort, then swung its head to look accusingly at Ichiro. He glared back.

"It's a graveyard," Ichiro said. "For all those who attempted to climb Heaven's Trail and failed." He wondered if Sensue had a pile of stones here, and what eulogy he would give if he found it.

"Umm," Daijiro glanced back the way they had come. "Maybe we should find somewhere else to sleep?"

The moon and stars were bright enough to paint the mountain in ethereal gloom, but not so bright they should risk continuing. And besides, Ichiro was exhausted. He let out an expansive yawn as he pulled his sword from his belt. Then he placed his back against a tree and settled down to sitting, laying his sword across his lap.

"We should be fine," he said around another yawn. "Just whatever you do, don't disturb any of the graves."

Daijiro glanced fretfully at the little stone piles. "Why not? You don't think there're ghosts, do you?"

Ichiro widened his eyes.

"Don't you mess with me, Aniki. Are you saying this place is haunted?"

Ichiro turned his smile a little sinister. "You're dragging a dead man up a mountain, and we've stopped in a graveyard full of the dead who tried to climb their way to heaven and failed. Good chance of ghosts, I reckon."

"I don't like ghosts!"

"Then don't disturb any graves."

They settled down, Daijiro sticking close to the donkey and keeping his spear in easy reach. It was a chilly night, so high up, but the sky was clear and the stars shone down on them like a million jewels. They shared the last of the food, Ichiro's remaining fish and a few rice balls Daijiro had tucked away.

"Where do you think he'll go when we set him free?" Daijiro asked, waving a hand at the tapestry of stars. It was a common belief that all those souls who made it to heaven joined the night sky as new stars to watch over their descendants.

"Who knows," Ichiro said. "But knowing Subaru, he won't be happy unless he's the brightest light up there. Arsehole!"

Daijiro chuckled and nodded. "Arsehole! You remember the night we all met?"

"Hard to forget. Worst day of my life," Ichiro lied with a smile.

"I walked into that tavern and it was like being hit by a blizzard. I'd never seen a man that drunk."

"Subaru was that drunk five days out of six."

Daijiro smiled up at the stars. "Sure. But I wasn't talking about him."

"I wasn't drunk! The arsehole had spilled his wine over me."

"You keep telling yourself that, Aniki. Way I saw it, sober as a desert, I might add, you were both swaying, spitting, snarling, and slurring."

Ichiro ground his teeth at the miss-telling. "I was quiet and composed, kneeling at my table as befit a warrior. Subaru was cavorting, standing on his table and shouting like a horny monkey."

"Pfft!" Daijiro snorted and the donkey joined in. "You were only kneeling because you were too drunk to stand."

"I was not!"

"What was it Subaru said? He nailed you with an insult that got you to draw steel on him."

"He said..." Ichiro glared at his little brother's body, laughed and shook his head. He couldn't be angry at something so long ago. "He said my father should have pissed before rutting my mother, not during, then they might have had a real son!"

"Piss baby!" Daijiro said, roaring with laughter. Ichiro sighed at the old nickname that had once been an insult, then turned a bizarre term of endearment between friends as close as brothers.

"Before you go recasting yourself as the sober hero of this memory, let's not forget why you were there, brother," Ichiro said. "Those soldiers were only ten steps behind you."

"I was innocent," Daijiro protested.

"Of all things you've been in your life, innocent was never one!"

"I was innocent from a certain point of view." Daijiro leaned back against the donkey's chest. It flicked its tail and grunted. "You might be right, Aniki. But you're the one who turned on them when they tried to take me. It was you who shouted you would *not allow a misapplication of authority in your presence, nor stand by while bucket-headed thugs dragged away a man whose only crime was not kissing the arse of some dreary-eyed coin stacker who'd never held a sword.*"

"I said that?" Ichiro asked.

"Well, you slurred it! Honestly, it was an impressive tirade from a man who couldn't kneel straight."

"I thought it was Subaru."

Daijiro shook his head. "He was the first to throw himself at the soldiers, but they were your words, Aniki. Subaru was always inspired by your words. We both were. You were always so passionate and so anti-establishment. It was hard not to get caught up in it."

Ichiro flexed his fingers, staring at the old calluses that had grown soft. "I've changed a lot."

"We all have. None of us are the young men we once were, full of fire. Take Subaru for instance. He used to be alive."

Ichiro chuckled at the morbid joke. Had he changed so much? He still believed in many of the same values, still hated the systems of rule and governance. But he no longer raised his sword against them. Instead, he taught others about the ills of the system.

Through the books he had his students study from, the texts he gave them to read. Still a rebel, a bandit, only now he fought in a different way.

Daijiro let out a cry of alarm and rolled to his feet, spear already in hand. "Ghosts!"

He wasn't wrong. Ethereal balls of blue light were rising from the graves, drifting about the plateau. The donkey raised its head, looked about, then sighed and went back to sleep.

"Ghosts," Daijiro repeated, waving his spear at one of the little fireballs that was coming close.

"They're harmless, brother," Ichiro said. He poked a finger at one and it was cool to the touch, but formless, like fingering powdery snow. It drifted back a little, then crowded in again, curious.

"But they are ghosts?"

"After a fashion. They're hitodama. Grave lights. The souls of the dead not deserving of hell, nor allowed into heaven, and too lost for rebirth, yet not vicious enough to become yokai. They drift around their graves, bound to their bones, losing more of themselves each day until they just fade away. Poor lost souls."

Daijiro grumbled as he waved away another of the hitodama. "Why are they coming towards me?"

"They're curious. You're alive, you remember yourself. They don't, so they're drawn to that." He wondered if Sensue was one of the lights, maybe even the one hovering near his face now, drawn to him, a fragment of her old life, without even understanding why.

"Close your eyes, brother. Ignore them and get some rest."

"Hah!" Daijiro barked. "No chance I'm sleeping with these creeps about."

"Suit yourself." Ichiro closed his eyes and drifted. He needed to sleep. Tomorrow they would cross the gap and climb the Koma mountain to the summit of the world. Tomorrow they would say goodbye to Subaru for good.

THE ONCE PROUD FORTRESS

Standing strong between.
Life behind but death ahead.
The gateway to hope.

Ichiro woke with the morning light. It blazed over the mountain tops like molten gold and set the sky on fire.

Despite his claims that he would never sleep with the ghost fires about, Daijiro was curled up with the donkey, snoring like a bear in winter. Ichiro decided to let his brother sleep a while longer, they would both need the rest for the journey ahead.

The hitodama were all gone. Grave lights always retreated to their remains before the sun came up. Ichiro walked across the plateau, picking his way through the graves and making certain not to disturb any. Once, he might have kicked a few over, just to be rebellious, just to challenge whatever might come for him. But he was not that angry youth anymore. Age had tempered him, given his rebellious spirit focus. Life had taught him to respect. He knelt in the centre of the plateau, surrounded by the graves, and bowed his head.

"I'm sorry, Sensue. Sorry that I left, instead of helping you complete your journey. Apparently I'm good at that, leaving when I'm needed most. I'm sorry that I was angry at you, for not telling me why you were in Ringen. I blamed you for the little time we had together. It was unfair of me to blame you for dying. I hope you made it, and this prayer of mine is for nothing. But if you didn't..." He leaned forward, pressed his hand to the stone, a single tear falling and eagerly swallowed by the ground. "I'm sorry."

When he got back to the cart, both Daijiro and the donkey were awake. "Time to go?" Daijiro asked.

Ichiro nodded. "Time to go grant this arsehole his last wish. It really is unfair that he dies and we have to carry him up the mountain."

Daijiro shrugged and slapped the donkey's flanks. "This poor bugger is doing most of the carrying."

They set out towards Lord Manamanto's gap, following the serpentine path. The going was easier than before, despite the rocky trail and wobbling cart wheel, and Ichiro realised they were on a slight descent towards the fort that bridged the gap.

"Do you remember that time Subaru tried to cook?" Daijiro asked.

"Thinking about food, brother?" They had run out of things to eat unless they started chewing on weeds like the donkey.

"Trying to take my mind off it."

"Remembering Subaru's cooking will definitely do that. He burned the rice."

"He burned everything. Even the fire!"

"How did he get to be an adult without learning how to cook rice?" Ichiro asked, glancing back at the body in its wrappings. Even the preserving herbs couldn't quite mask the smell of decay anymore.

"I guess he never needed to," Daijiro said. "Told me he grew up in the forest, never even saw a village until he was ten."

"So? You grew up in the wilds, too, brother."

"Me? Nah. I grew up in Kodachi, Aniki. Spent my childhood on the streets, bouncing between whichever gang wouldn't kick the crap out of me that day. Learning to cook early was a good way to convince them I was useful."

"But not fish?"

"I hate fish," Daijiro said. "Tastes like mushy, salty water. I just wonder, do you think Subaru ever learned? After we went our separate ways and he was on his own again, he might have learned to cook. Or maybe he didn't, and now he'll never get the chance."

Ichiro glanced at the body again. He knew the truth. Subaru would never have learned to cook because he didn't need to. Ichiro knew that because he knew what Subaru had done after they all split up. He knew what their little brother had made of himself. Or maybe what *she* had turned him into.

Lord Manamanto's gap was a vast valley gouged between two mountains like a ragged blade had cut through earth and rock. Below it rushed the largest, most violent river Ichiro had ever seen, and the roar of the water could be heard even so high above. That river eventually opened out into a few hundred of the Thousand Falls, but here it was condensed into a vast and savage thing. Dauntless trees clinging to near sheer rock faces dotted the valley walls in stubborn smudges of green on the otherwise grey rock.

Spanning the valley from one mountain to another was a crumbling old bridge fortress. It had once been mighty enough that Ichiro could not understand how it had been built, at least not by mortal hands, but disrepair and the decaying touch of age and weather had turned the stone to treacherous crumble, the walls to dilapidated ruin, and the old doors to mouldering planks of rotting wood. Vines clung to the walls, many of them dangling over the vast drop below. He'd heard the fortress had once housed a hundred soldiers, and the fortifications on each side of the gap meant those hundred could hold the fort against ten thousand from either side. But those glory days were gone along with the soldiers. Now, it sat abandoned, a crumbling ruin that looked likely to fall away beneath their feet.

There were a dozen old tents, flapping as the wind blew through them, staked before the fortress walls. Ichiro peered into a few, but they were cold and bare, as abandoned as the fort.

“I don't know about you, Aniki,” Daijiro said as they approached the old gate that opened onto the bridge. “But I am getting pretty serious *bad shit happened here* vibes.”

The donkey snorted in a way that sounded a lot like 'too right'.

“The way forward is over the bridge,” Ichiro said. “The only way forward. We could turn back.”

Daijiro frowned. “No. Onwards, I guess. I'm just saying... bad shit vibes.”

They crossed under the grand arch of the gateway where rocky mountain became stone bridge. The disrepair was even worse from inside. The entire left side of the bridge fort had long ago given way and now ended in a jigsaw of stone blocks, open to the air. A series of wooden braces held the right-side wall up. The wind howled and whisked around the fortress, tugging at the folds of Ichiro's haori this way and that. For once, he was jealous of Daijiro's furs.

“I take back the bad shit vibes,” Daijiro said. “This place has trap written all over it.”

As if to answer his accusation, the great wooden door behind them squealed on its hinges as it swung ponderously closed. Ichiro saw men on the other side through gaps in the rotting wood. The clomp of many boots filled the fort, competing with the wind, as a dozen rough-looking men and women rushed out of the surviving fortress buildings. Three took up positions on the right-side wall, short bows held ready, while others arrayed themselves on the bridge before Ichiro and Daijiro. A small warband worth of bandits, and warbands went nowhere without a chief. Two more men sauntered onto the bridge. The chieftain was obvious; he was a big man with oily hair and pitted cheeks, and he was wearing a scratched up suit of ceramic plate armour, painted a fading orange, while the rest of his bandits were wearing an assortment of furs, rags, and filth.

"Well, what have we here?" shouted the chief, his voice booming. "The mighty Brothers Blood. I knew we'd meet again."

Ichiro squinted at the man across the bridge.

"You do that a lot these days," Daijiro said.

"Do what?" Ichiro asked.

Daijiro's face pinched like a squirrel as he made an exaggerated squint.

"He's a good thirty paces away."

Daijiro shrugged. "I'm just saying, maybe you need glasses. You are getting old."

"It's fitting," the chief bellowed, "that I get to take my vengeance on you here."

"Do you recognise him?" Ichiro asked.

"Which one?" Daijiro said.

"The ugly one."

Daijiro glanced about and shook his head. "You're gonna have to be a lot more specific."

Ichiro pointed at the man beside the chief. "See the one with no nose?"

"Shit! He IS the ugly one."

"Well, the big fellow beside him."

Daijiro's jaw dropped. "That's a bloke? I thought it was your mother."

Ichiro turned to his brother. "What?"

Daijiro chuckled. "Never seen him before, Aniki."

Ichiro took a step forward. "We don't know you. We have nothing to steal. We're just trying—"

"My mother was Lady Silence!" the chief roared.

"Shit!" Ichiro said.

"I knew that would come back to bite us one day," Daijiro said.

"Fitting that it only bites us after Subaru is dead."

"What does that mean?" Daijiro asked with a frown.

Ichiro cursed himself for almost letting the secret slip. "Not the time, brother."

"Right, right. Time to get serious." Daijiro reached into the cart and pulled out his spear.

"Last chance to let us pass," Ichiro said, thumbing his katana out of its saya.

The chief snarled. "A hundred lien to whoever strikes the killing blow!"

As one, the bandits roared and charged while the three archers along the wall moved to get a good line of sight. Ichiro hated archers.

There was a shout from above as one bandit behind them leapt down on Daijiro. The two men collided in a heap, but Ichiro couldn't spare them the attention.

He ran to meet the charging warband, and whipped his katana out of its saya, holding it in one hand.

"Six Element Style: Dance of Air." The first man to reach him had a squinty eye and a broad iron sword. Ichiro ducked under Squinty's slice and moved past him, dragging his katana across the man's leg, gouging a wound in his thigh. Squinty screamed and collapsed, and Ichiro moved on.

A tiny fellow with a rusty wakizashi in hand leapt for him. He drove the short blade at Ichiro but met only air as Ichiro spun away, lashing out with his katana and scoring a shallow cut down Titch's arm.

A red faced woman with a naginata was a poor match for Dance of Air, so Ichiro feinted low, then leapt back, turned, and sprinted for another opponent. Tomato Face growled and gave chase.

This was the strength of Dance of Air; fighting multiple opponents on the move. It relied on constant movement, shallow cuts, debilitating rather than killing.

Two men tried to pen Ichiro in, one with a wolfish snarl, and the other with an old burn scar across his face. Wolfy swung low, while Burns went high. Ichiro stepped into Wolfy's strike, brushed his blade away, then slammed his elbow into the man's snarl. He thrust out and stabbed Burns in the shoulder, pulled his sword free with a twist, then kicked Wolfy in the chest, using the force to propel him into a roll underneath the approaching Noseless' swinging chui. The spiked mace passed over Ichiro's head and slammed into Wolfy's chest, putting him down for good.

Noseless turned and barrelled after Ichiro, his spiked chui in constant motion, a poor match for a katana. Ichiro gave ground again and again in smooth but erratic steps to avoid prediction. He saw Noseless glance at something behind him. Ichiro turned just as Tomato Face slashed for him with a cut that would cleave him in two. Ichiro stopped his movement dead and knelt.

Even the wind took a breath sometimes.

His sudden stop worked and he saw the naginata blade pass an inch from his face, and felt Noseless' chui swipe the empty air where his head had been.

Before either of them could recover, Ichiro exploded forward, driving his hilt into Tomato Face's gut, then stabbing down, cleaving her foot in two, before spinning around her and pushing her into the path of Noseless who snarled and shoved the injured woman away.

A sharp whistle echoed over the howling wind and Noseless backed up a step. Ichiro leapt backwards just as three arrows flew at him. He avoided two, but the third sliced across his thigh and he almost collapsed, gritting his teeth against the sharp pain. It was a shallow cut, but a wound all the same. Noseless was already on him again, swinging his chui, forcing Ichiro to retreat.

"How are you doing, Aniki?" Daijiro bellowed. He had one man down at his feet, bleeding from a hundred little cuts, and was facing three more, keeping them at bay with range.

"I HATE archers!" Ichiro shouted.

Noseless kept advancing, giving him no space. Tomato Face was hopping forward, trying to get around Ichiro to attack him from behind.

Another whistle cut through the air.

"Errant Gust," Ichiro said, slicing his sword through the air. The wind coalesced into a gale just as the arrows loosed. It pulled them off course and they flew past Ichiro and impacted with a wet thud.

Everyone stopped for a moment as Tomato Face teetered on her feet. She looked down at the three arrows jutting from her chest, then back up at the archers. "Why me?" She collapsed sideways and didn't get up.

Noseless glowered, which Ichiro had to admit was quite scary on a face with no nose. The man charged him and Ichiro backed up, tripped over Red Face's body, and fell. He rolled away just as the chui crashed down, making absolutely certain Tomato Face was all sorts of dead.

Ichiro launched to his feet and sprinted away. He heard another whistle and swept his sword. "Updraft!" The wind rushed again, catching the loosed arrows and taking them over his head. He heard Noseless grunt in pain. Then Ichiro ran into the gusting wind and leapt. The updraft caught him and launched him thirty feet into the air, soaring across the bridge right towards the archers.

He slammed into the first archer which, luckily for him, arrested his momentum, but unluckily for the archer transferred it all to him. The man careened away over the side of the wall into the long, long drop of the valley below.

With a growl, Ichiro sliced his sword at the next archer. The swarthy woman tried to block with her bow, which was about as effective as stopping a rockslide with a rude gesture. His blade cleaved the bow, and her face in two.

The final archer held up his bow in one hand. "I surrender."

Ichiro rammed his katana into the man's chest and plucked the bow from his dying hands.

"Right then, let's see how you bastards like archers."

A bandit was running for the steps. Ichiro knocked, drew, and loosed in one fluid motion and the man died with an arrow in his neck.

"Uh oh! Guess who's trained with a bow. Who's next?"

From his vantage, Ichiro could see the entire bridge. The chief stood motionless, wide- eyed and slack jawed. Noseless was limping for cover, an arrow in his leg. Daijiro had three bandits held at bay. And one more bandit was menacing the donkey, trying to get to the cart it was hitched to.

"Hey! Get away from our donkey!" Ichiro roared and sent an arrow into the man's chest. He collapsed forwards, spitting blood and the donkey bit him in the crotch.

He turned his attention to Noseless and put an arrow in the man's gut. Noseless grunted in pain, but kept going. Ichiro put two more arrows into the man before he finally fell, but even then he kept crawling, which Ichiro had to admit was bloody impressive even if it was futile.

That left a bunch of wounded bandits downed and crawling for cover, the shell-shocked chief, and the three facing Daijiro. Ichiro put one of the three down with an arrow in the back.

Daijiro grinned. "Time to unleash my ultimate technique," he shouted, twirling his spear dramatically. "Infinite blade of folding darkness."

The two bandits glanced at each other, turned, and ran. Daijiro roared in laughter. "Hey, Aniki, you were right. It works."

Ichiro sighed and shook his head at his brother's foolishness. Then he put an arrow through the ankle of one of the fleeing men, dropping him. The final bandit made it to cover, pulling the chief down with him so they were both crouching behind a flapping tent. Ichiro was out of arrows anyway. He tossed the bow over the wall. He really hated those things.

Ichiro made for the steps as Daijiro moved across the bridge, calmly finishing the wounded bandits with clean spear thrusts to the chest.

"You got a bit angry up there," Daijiro said as Ichiro joined him on the bridge.

"I really hate archers. Cowards, all of them."

"I seem to remember Subaru favoured the bow."

Ichiro rolled his eyes. "My statement stands."

"Our brother was many things, but coward was never one of them."

Ichiro had to concede that point. "Infinite Spear of Dark whatever?"

"What? It sounded very scary and legitimate," Daijiro said.

"It's not about scaring them." He sighed. "It's about honour."

Daijiro patted him on the shoulder. "Sure. Sure. You're a very honourable old bandit, Aniki."

They stopped a few feet away from the tent where the two surviving bandits, including the chief, were hiding. "You regretting your life choices yet?" Daijiro asked loudly.

"We accept your deal!" the chief shouted back, still hiding behind the tent.

Ichiro glanced at Daijiro who just shrugged. "What deal?"

"We will let you pass unmolested. We won't steal anything from you."

"How magnanimous of you," Daijiro said.

Ichiro cleared his throat. "Given the recent attack, I no longer find your terms acceptable."

The bandit chief was quiet a moment. "Lady Silence will have her vengeance, Brothers Blood. If not today, then one day!" The man broke cover into a sprint, pulling the canvas of the tent behind him. Then he leapt over the ruined side of the bridge.

Both Ichiro and Daijiro stared in shock for a few seconds, then rushed to the edge to watch the fool fall to his death. They were hundreds of feet above the valley floor, and there was nothing but a roaring river below.

The bandit chief plummeted, wrestling with the canvas from the tent, then it bloomed out above him into a parachute, slowing his deadly fall to a drifting descent.

"I can't believe that worked," said a thin voice. Ichiro glanced to find the last remaining bandit standing next to Daijiro, staring agape.

They watched the chief drift down, down, down, then plop into the churning rapids. "You think he'll survive that?" Daijiro asked.

"Knowing our luck," Ichiro said.

"I have a feeling that's going to come back on us one day."

Ichiro turned to the last bandit. "And what should we do with you?"

The young man had a mop of oily, dark hair, and a strip of a moustache. He grinned for a moment, then bolted. Ichiro and Daijiro watched the young bandit run past the bodies of his fallen comrades and slam into the rotting door. He shoved his shoulder against it over and over again.

"Think we should help?" Daijiro asked.

"It is better to show discretion in the face of victory, than honour at the feet of defeat," Ichiro said.

Daijiro shook his head. "Nope. That one was awful."

Ichiro cleared his throat. "Ok, how about: Never let a gruesome defeat stand in the way of a lesson sorely learned."

"Try again."

The maxim was on the tip of his tongue, he just couldn't quite remember it.

"Those who, uh, think to run away..." He hung his head in shame. "Learn to live another day."

Daijiro clapped. "That's it! He's got it. Sage wisdom."

"That was a bloody children's rhyme."

Daijiro draped his arm across Ichiro's shoulders. "And children can be exceedingly wise. Come on, Aniki. Let's loot this fortress, eh? I am hungry enough to eat the stone."

An hour later, they'd feasted on stale, salted horse strips, had loaded the cart with as much food as they could fit around Subaru's preserved corpse, and had broken open the rotting gate. Koma mountain stretched up before them and at the peak, Ichiro could just about make out the great shrine. It was the last leg of their journey and his knees were already aching in anticipation of the trip back down.

THE SPIRIT OF THE MOUNTAIN

Sacrifice honour.
The path forward now demands.
Truth lies in the fury.

PAST THE FORT, THE TRAIL GREW STEEP AND ROCKY, SO every footstep was a climb. Ichiro's wounded leg ached from the effort, but he persevered. He had no choice. The wound was not too serious and he had taken far worse before. It stung though and he had to admit, he was no longer used to getting hurt.

They lashed Subaru's body to the cart with some rope they'd taken from the fort, and all the while, the donkey eyed them sullenly. Ichiro walked at the donkey's head, ready to encourage it on if needed, and eyed the wobbling cart wheel, hoping it would hold together until they reached the summit.

As the trail wound around the mountain, they lost sight of Lord Manamanto's gap and the ruined fort. This side of the mountain, all they could see was the jagged peaks of the Oka mountain range, dusted in white and endless as an ocean. It made the Ipian empire feel like a small thing, being so high up. As though, if they just climbed far enough, all the troubles of humanity became inconsequential. Perhaps that was why the gods were so uninterested in worldly affairs, because heaven gave them such distance that human squabbles became trivial things. Then again, maybe they had other problems to deal with. If the stories were to be believed, gods squabbled, tricked, and warred amongst themselves as regularly as mortals. Perhaps that was what the distance of heaven bought the gods, a detachment from worldly woes to worry about their own instead. Just like an Ipian farmer didn't care how a Hosan man's crops were growing, because he had his own field to tend. All distance ever really accomplished, was to make other people seem small.

Ichiro slapped a hand across his face to dash away the melancholy. He and Daijiro had lapsed into silence, and it was making him philosophical again. He'd been alone but for his students for a long time. Too long. He was too used to stewing in his own thoughts. Isolationism made philosophy stale. Like any good dish, a truly significant piece of wisdom needed ingredients from many minds.

Up ahead, Daijiro sucked in a deep breath. "Mmm. Smell that fresh mountain air, Aniki."

Ichiro drew in a breath, and the sour shit stench hit him like a knee to the crotch. He choked on it, coughing. "Was that you?" he sputtered, trying not to gag.

Daijiro patted his belly. "That horse meat is making itself known, brother."

"Gah! You smell worse than the donkey, Daijiro."

Daijiro stretched his hands above his head. "Speaking of the donkey. Don't think I didn't hear that back at the fort. *Get away from our donkey!* And I thought you hated the poor beast."

Ichiro glanced at the animal. It met his gaze and twitched its ears.

"I hated one donkey, which I'm still not certain ever was a donkey."

"It looked like a donkey."

"It talked!" Ichiro said. "Donkeys don't talk."

"Unless they do, but just don't think you're very good at listening."

The donkey let out a bray that sounded too much like a laugh.

"It's not that I dislike this donkey, I just distrust it. Besides, I didn't want to carry Subaru's body up the mountain myself."

"But you would have?" Daijiro said. "Carried him, I mean. If you had to."

"Of course. Though I'd hope you would at least take a turn."

Daijiro smiled, not mockingly, but a happy smile, and turned back to the trail.

The mountain grew misty as they passed into a layer of cloud. Frost coated the ground, turning to a sprinkle of snow, then a thin blanket that soaked into Ichiro's boots and made his toes numb. The donkey soldiered on, dragging the cart through the snow, but its breath huffed and steamed. The clouds became so thick they could only see a dozen feet ahead. The trail became treacherous, as though the closer they got, the more the mountain itself resisted their progress.

They were about an hour into their trek through the clouds when Daijiro shouted for them to stop. He was ranging a few steps ahead, using his spear to check the footing beneath the snow. Ichiro walked up beside his brother and pulled the cart to a halt. The donkey huffed gratefully and sat in the snow. The trail here was narrow, only large enough for two carts to pass. On one side, the mountain rose steeply into a near vertical climb, and on the other it dropped into a perilous patch of snowy scree. And in the centre of the trail was a great boulder that blocked it off.

"This is going to make things difficult," Daijiro said, rubbing a hand across his forehead.

Ichiro stared thoughtfully at the boulder. Something was off. It sat too perfectly on the trail, and while snow coated the ground, there was none on the boulder itself. But it couldn't have so recently fallen onto the path or they would have heard it.

Daijiro shuffled to the edge of the trail and stared down at the scree. He shook his head. "No way past. Can you... Foundations of Earth this thing?"

Ichiro scratched his chin as he considered. The elemental techniques associated with the Foundations of Earth style were suited to moving rocks, but he'd never shifted anything so large before. And the last thing they needed was for him to accidentally trigger an avalanche. He approached the boulder and placed a hand to it. It was strangely warm and rippled at his touch.

Ichiro leapt backwards, hand flying to his katana. "That's no rock!"

The boulder shifted, the surface rippling and changing and lifting. A great bald head with a shaggy white beard swung into view, and an eye as big as Ichiro's head opened and blinked a few times before focusing on them.

The giant groaned as he lumbered about. The trail shook as he moved and pebbles rattled down from above. He stood and the ratty old cloak they had thought was stone hung awkwardly on the massive body. The giant loomed at least three times the height of a man. His legs were thin, with coarse black hairs, and each foot was as big as the cart, each toe ending in a curled yellow nail like a talon. He had stooped shoulders and a bulging pot belly, with long arms that hung almost to the ground.

"Do we fight?" Daijiro asked as he backed up, spear held at the ready. The donkey was trying to reverse, but the cart was stuck.

"I don't think so," Ichiro said, peeling his hand from his katana. "I think this is a kami. It's the spirit of Koma mountain."

The kami were not quite gods, but they weren't far off either. They were forces of nature, perhaps even more dangerous than any one god, and certainly more unpredictable. This was the kami of the very mountain they stood upon, and that meant its power here was absolute.

"What do we do?" Daijiro asked.

Ichiro winced as he considered and discarded *run the crap away* as an option. "We beg for a boon?"

He raised his hands to show they were empty of weapon, and stepped forward. "Great kami of the mountain."

The giant's great head swivelled about as it looked at him, then it scuttled forward unnervingly fast and bent down. The kami sniffed him in three long breaths. Up close, the spirit smelled earthy, almost metallic. It had huge, crooked yellow teeth in its mouth, and its pale grey eyes swirled like a blizzard. Its head swung to Daijiro and it sniffed again. Daijiro went rigid, his knuckles white on his spear.

"No threatening moves," Ichiro warned quietly.

"Threatening?" the kami said, its voice high and reedy. It rocked back on the balls of its massive feet and laughed. The entire mountain seemed to shake with the laughter. "What would be threatening?"

"We just wish to pass, great kami."

"Pass? Hmm." It rocked back and forth again and pebbles cascaded down from above. Its giant head darted about like a bird. "They used to come. They used to pass, but never so empty." It flexed one of its great, gnarled hands towards them.

"We're on our way to the summit," Ichiro explained. "To the shrine. To send our brother to heaven." He motioned towards the cart.

The giant looked at the cart and his maelstrom eyes went wide. "Oh! Not empty." It lurched forward on hands and feet, pot belly dragging on the snowy ground, and reached a great hand between Ichiro and Daijiro. "A snack!"

The cart burst apart under the kami's huge hand. The donkey brayed in panic as the giant snatched up Subaru's body and pulled it back. The kami's jaw snapped and cracked as it distended like a snake's and it lowered Subaru's body into its mouth.

"No!" Ichiro and Daijiro shouted together, both rushing forward a couple of steps.

The kami paused, Subaru's corpse half in its mouth.

"Not a snack!" Daijiro hissed. "Not food. He's our brother, you stupid spirit... thing."

The kami pulled Subaru away and then its jaw snapped back into position. "Not brother," it said. "Empty. See. Empty." It shook the body violently in its hand.

"Please, great kami," Ichiro said. "Put our brother down."

The kami shook the body again and Ichiro heard bones snapping. "Brother. Brother. Brother. Not brother." It leaned forward, staring at Ichiro. "I see your heart. You hated him."

Daijiro turned towards Ichiro. "What's it talking about?"

Ichiro glanced at Daijiro, winced, and turned back to the kami. "Of course I hated him from time to time. He was an arsehole. But he was my brother."

"Not by blood," said the kami.

"No. By something deeper than blood. He was my brother by kinship. By choice. By battles fought, those won and those lost. We faced the world side by side, together, time after time, and we always watched each others' backs. We didn't have blood between us, because we had trust and we had love.

"So, yes, I hated Subaru a little, especially towards the end. But he was my brother and I will not let you eat him!"

"What do you mean you hated him towards the end, Ichiro?" Daijiro asked.

Ichiro glanced at him. "Not the time."

The kami waited, massive head twitching as it looked between them. It still held Subaru's corpse away from them, like a child afraid someone would take away their favourite toy.

"Seems like a good time to me," Daijiro said. "You never told me why you left. Subaru never told me either. So, why did you leave, Ichiro?"

Ichiro didn't want Daijiro to know, especially not now Subaru was gone and it didn't matter anymore. He wanted his brother's memory of Subaru to remain perfect, unmarred by the damning truth.

"Kami, please give us our brother back."

"Answer me, Ichiro," Daijiro shouted. "What happened between you and Subaru? Why did you leave?"

"Because he betrayed us!" Ichiro snapped. "Subaru betrayed the brotherhood. What we stood for."

Daijiro just stared at him, his face hard and impassive. And now the truth had started to slip out, Ichiro had no choice. Either he told his brother everything, or he risked losing him, too.

Ichiro felt a nudge against his leg and looked down to see the donkey, no doubt snuffling for food. He was a little surprised it hadn't already run away and he swatted at it to shoo it off.

It was time for the whole truth to come out. "Subaru was working for the Lotus Maiden."

Daijiro opened his mouth, but Ichiro cut him off.

"I know we were all working for her, but not like this. We formed the Brothers Blood to fight back against authority. To steal from the rich. To prove to the wealthy families they weren't safe. And to stick a thumb in the eyes of the imperial regime. We were rebels. Outlaws. Bandits adhering to the true code. We had honour. Until the bloody Lotus Maiden stripped it from us.

"You know what she made us do. The things she ordered us to steal, the assassinations, the other gangs we destroyed for her." Ichiro grit his teeth and shook his head. "Lady Silence should have been our ally, she knew every dirty little secret of every lord and lady in Kodachi. But when we stole her Book of Truths, we destroyed Lady Silence. Not because she opposed what we stood for, but because the Lotus Maiden wanted her gone, and wanted the one thing that kept her powerful.

"At first, I thought it was only a matter of time. We would find a way to free ourselves from her clutches. But month after month, Subaru brought us more jobs from her, until that was all he brought. Until we stopped being the Brothers Blood and became just another one of her thug gangs, hunting down her enemies. Subaru did that to us! And every month I looked for a way out, he just dug us further in.

"I know he was sleeping with the evil bitch, but I didn't realise how tight her claws were on his balls. And when I confronted him about it, Subaru told me I didn't know what I was talking about and I should just back off and let him handle it. He said the big decisions weren't meant for mid-level grunts like me."

Ichiro staggered back a step and sighed. He was exhausted and trembling, as though holding the secret in had been the only thing keeping him upright. The kami stood there, Subaru's corpse all but forgotten in its huge hand. Daijiro was frowning, silent for once in his life. The donkey sniffled at Ichiro's leg again. He swatted it on the nose.

"Subaru betrayed everything we stood for," Ichiro said quietly. "He made us into puppets, working for a master who strove to prop up the very systems we wanted to bring down. So I left because the only alternative I could see would have ended in blood."

Daijiro shook his head. "Ichiro, you're wrong. Subaru wasn't working for the Lotus Maiden. He was the Lotus Maiden."

Ichiro opened his mouth, then shut it, trying to make sense of the words. He tried again. "What?"

Daijiro gave him the same look Ichiro gave his students when they failed to grasp a simple task. "Subaru *was* the Lotus Maiden."

Ichiro shook his head. "No. N—no. Because we fought against the Lotus Maiden. Together. She almost killed us. All three of us."

"True, but that was the original Lotus Maiden. And I can't argue with you, she was a real evil fish. We all knew that. Subaru knew it just as well as you. But he found the way out you never could. You know how charming Subaru could be. He seduced the Maiden, slept with her, then killed her in her sleep and took her place."

"Huh?" Ichiro tried to imagine it. His little brother, always so full of smiles, who often smelled like the backside of a goat, and had once tripped over his own shadow. And the Lotus Maiden, her cold, sharp, painted face, who always smelled of jasmine, never met a smile she didn't first slit, then dissect, and who carried so many knives she even had them tied into her braided hair. He just couldn't see it.

"How?" Ichiro sat in the snow next to the donkey.

Daijiro came and squatted before him. "I already told you, he was good at pretending to be a woman long before we ran into the Maiden. He knew we'd never wriggle out from under her, so to speak, so he hatched a plan to become her instead.

"Then, all that about us fighting authority and sticking it to the powerful. We were! Just, we were doing it for her. Or him as her, I suppose. We gutted the crime bosses that preyed on the weak, robbed from the wealthy, and undermined the nobility. We just did it as thugs of the Lotus Maiden, not as the Brothers Blood. He used Lady Silence's Book of Truths to control wealthy business owners, gave the power to worker unions. You just didn't see it, brother, because you were too focused on trying to get out from under her."

Ichiro was still trying to get his head around it all. "Why didn't he tell me?"

"Ichiro, can you honestly say you'd have understood? Not just him taking her place, but that he felt more comfortable being the Lotus Maiden, more comfortable as a woman, than he ever was in his own skin."

"I... I might have."

"Ichiro," Daijiro said, shaking his head.

Ichiro looked up at the wrapped corpse of Subaru, still clutched in the kami's grip. "I didn't really know him at all, did I? Who was he?"

"Of course you knew him," Daijiro said sharply. "He was our brother. No matter what clothes he wore, or what he called himself, he was our brother. He still is, even gone."

Ichiro buried his head in his hands, unable to meet Daijiro's gaze. "I ruined everything. *I* destroyed the brotherhood and walked away, all for a lie, a... ruse. All those years we lost, that you spent in the fighting pits, that Subaru was alone. It's all my fault."

Daijiro snorted. "That's enough of the self pity, Aniki. You don't get to shoulder all the blame. If Subaru hadn't been such a prideful arsehole, you and he might have figured it out. I chose to go looking for you, and if I hadn't been drunk as a monk on worship day, I would never have been caught. Blame sits on three sides here, including his dead shoulders, so don't eat the whole hog yourself."

Ichiro nodded numbly. He felt ragged as a ripped cloth.

"You want to make it up to Subaru, then stand up and let's get him the rest of the way up there," Daijiro said. "Because no matter what happened between us all, no matter who we became afterwards. When he knew he was dying, he made sure *we* would be the ones to carry him. He trusted us to get him to heaven, and I don't mean to let our little brother down. So. Get. Up."

Daijiro stood and held out his hand. Ichiro stared at it for a moment, still wallowing in his despair, but Daijiro was right. About everything. But also that out of all those Subaru had come to know since the three of them split up, the only ones he trusted to get him to heaven, were his brothers. Ichiro took Daijiro's hand and felt the donkey nudge him. Between the three of them, they got him back to his feet.

"Alright." Ichiro sniffed and wiped at his eyes. "Alright. Great kami, we're going to need our brother back now."

The kami had been watching them, fascinated and still as stone but for the twitching of its head. Now it looked at Subaru's body and lowered it, laying him down on the trampled snow. Judging by the awkward bulges in the funeral shawl, the spirit's manhandling had done some damage to the body, but Ichiro didn't think Subaru would mind as long as there was still enough of him to burn at the summit.

"Empty offerings," the kami said. "Empty. Empty. Empty. Many travellers come. But none pass empty." It slammed a palm onto the ground with each of the last three words, and the mountain shook with each impact.

"Another offering?" Daijiro said. "Monks and bandits, spirits and whatever this thing is. How many do we have to pay just to climb a bloody mountain?"

"Make your offering," the kami said, looming over them. Ichiro had a feeling they'd only get the one chance.

"Fine," Daijiro said, reaching into his furs. "I took some lien from the bandits. How much do you want?"

Ichiro held out his hand to stop Daijiro. "The kami doesn't want coin, brother. It wants something valuable."

"Uh..." Daijiro jingled the little pouch of lien in his hand.

"Real value comes not from society's perceived worth, but from an individual's desire to withhold."

Daijiro nodded. "Very philosophical. That was a good one."

"Thanks. I just thought of it."

"What's it mean?"

Ichiro sighed. "Something of value is something it hurts to give up."

"Ohhh," Daijiro said. "I have grown quite fond of the donkey."

The donkey gnashed its teeth at Daijiro, which struck Ichiro as a little strange because a donkey should not have understood him.

"I'm not carrying Subaru's corpse up the rest of the mountain," Ichiro said. "You?"

"Good point. What else do we have?"

Ichiro shook his head. He had nothing but the clothes on his back and the memories in his head, and he wouldn't give those up no matter what. But there was one other thing he had. Something he had carried with him most of his life. Something as much a part of him as his hands, his mind, or his heart.

Ichiro took a step towards the great kami, and pulled his katana from his belt, still sheathed in its saya.

Daijiro gasped. "Aniki, no."

Ichiro shook his head at his brother. This was his choice to make.

"Great kami, I offer you my sword. Commissioned by my father. Forged by the smith Hancho. Given to me the day I turned a man. The sword is the soul of the warrior, but if this is the price of seeing my brother to rest, then I pay it gladly."

The kami shifted, leaning forward. Its huge, swirling eyes peered at the sword, then it sniffed again. "Good metal," it said in its reedy voice. "Many lives it has taken. Much blood has washed its steel."

The kami reached out a craggy hand and plucked the sword from Ichiro's fingers. It was almost painful, letting it go, and Ichiro had to stop himself from snatching it back. But his choice was made. It was worth it. For Subaru.

"Your offer is accepted," the kami said. It lifted Ichiro's sword, opened its mouth, then swallowed the blade.

Ichiro started forward before he knew what he was doing. He lifted a hand, but it was too late. "You ate it? You ate my sword?"

The kami of the mountain patted a craggy hand against its belly, then turned and lumbered away into the clouds. Within seconds, it was gone.

Ichiro felt a hand on his shoulder as Daijiro stepped up beside him. His brother sniffed, and there were tears in his eyes. "A grand sacrifice, Aniki. You've always been an example I could never hope to match."

Ichiro turned stricken eyes on his brother. "It ate my sword!"

THE TEMPLE AT THE TOP OF THE WORLD

One life and one death.
Watching past, present, future.
Last of guardians.

THEY LASHED SUBARU'S BODY TO THE DONKEY. IT huffed in annoyance, but Ichiro batted it on the head until it quieted. It was only there to carry the corpse, and cart or no cart, that was what it would do. Even wrapped in the funeral shawl, the body flopped about, and Ichiro hoped they'd reach the summit soon.

The donkey wasn't the only one off balance. He felt strange without his sword, lopsided and uncoordinated. He kept trying to rest his hand on a hilt that wasn't there. He wondered what his father would say if he knew. First Ichiro had given away his pride, then his name and heritage, and now his sword. He knew his father would disapprove, but he had always disapproved of everything

Ichiro had done. Still, it was a price Ichiro would pay a hundred times over, even knowing that the kami would eat the sword.

They passed through the clouds as the trail closed in on the mountain summit. A peach-coloured sky awaited them, climbing to near white before it gave way to the stars. It felt like they were alone in the world, the clouds a crumpled white blanket like an ocean of cotton, and the mountain they stood on was the only thing breaching it. They stood upon the top of the world, and for the first time, Ichiro found himself actually believing in the ritual. Perhaps they really could send Subaru to heaven here, where the stars met the earth and the gods felt close enough to reach out and touch.

The summit looked like it had been flattened, and stone slabs were laid out in a wide courtyard leading up to a squat temple. Frost covered the ground, but the air was strangely still, barely a breath of wind as though the elements themselves were paying respect.

They passed through an old red toori and into the courtyard. A feeling of intense anticipation thrummed through Ichiro's blood. They were almost there. They were almost finished.

"No more climbing," Daijiro said. "I cannot explain how happy this makes my knees."

"You know we still have to go back down yet?"

Daijiro scowled at him. "Shut up!"

The temple was wood and painted white and gold, strangely well-preserved given the location. It boasted just two floors, the upper one open to the sky and the lower shielded only by paper doors. In front of the temple, flanking the steps leading up to it were two stone shishi statues. Each one was twice as large as a horse with the body of a lion and the head of a dog. The statue on the left of the shrine had its mouth open in a growl, while the statue on the right's mouth was closed. The temple guardians were common enough in front of shrines all over Ipia, but Ichiro had never thought to see such craftsmanship here.

"Come on then, Subaru," Daijiro said. "I'm sick of carrying your body around."

The donkey gave its tail a flick of annoyance. Ichiro smiled and followed them, staring up at the sky.

A grating of stone was all the warning they got, then the close-mouthed shishi statue pounced. Daijiro got his spear up just in time to stop it crushing him, but the statue still slammed him down against the frosty stone and dragged him back and forth. The donkey shrieked in alarm and ran for the edge of the courtyard.

Ichiro ran to his brother's aid and reached for his... His hand fell where his sword hilt should be. "Shit!"

A stone paw slammed into Ichiro from the side and he was flung away to hit the ground hard, rolling to a painful stop.

As he climbed back to his feet, Ichiro heard metal ringing on stone. Daijiro was up, stabbing at the statue as it stalked after the donkey. The shishi cavorted, leaping about, and its tail whipped out, taking Daijiro's legs out from under him. The statue then sprang after the donkey, which screamed in panic again and bolted away. Ichiro ran to his brother and hauled him up. Daijiro shouted in pain as he put weight on his left leg.

"Nothing broken, but ow!"

"What's it doing?" Ichiro said.

The donkey was charging about, Subaru's corpse flopping on its back. The statue was chasing it, trying to bring it down with crushing paw strikes.

"It's going after Subaru," Daijiro said. He winced as he took a couple of experimental limps. "The closed mouth shishi represents death, the end. It's the final guardian."

"We have to stop it," Ichiro said, no idea how to go about it.

"A masterful point, Aniki. No wonder we followed you. Here."

Daijiro reached into his furs and pulled out a small knife, handing it to Ichiro.

"What am I supposed to do with this?" Ichiro asked, turning the finger-long blade about in his hands.

"You know, clean its nails, maybe tickle its balls. STAB IT!"

"It's made of stone!"

"Then stab it really hard!"

They glared at each other for a moment while the donkey charged around screaming, chased by a giant stone statue.

"Alright, I have an idea," Ichiro said.

"Wonderful, will it work?"

"Probably not."

"Even better. What do I do?" Daijiro asked.

Ichiro pointed to where the donkey was backed against the temple wall, the shishi closing on it. "Protect our brother for a minute."

"Got it!" Daijiro twirled his spear and limped towards the shishi. "Hey, ugly, let's dance!" He struck like a viper, slashing at the statue's flanks, dragging its attention away from the donkey.

Ichiro held the little knife and concentrated on his form. He had no idea if it would work. He'd never tried a sword form with a blade so small, nor tried the fifth element while above the clouds.

"Six Element Style: Rage of Lightning." He settled onto the balls of his feet, body side long to his target, and brought the knife down to his side as if it were sheathed in a saya. This was the form of lightning. Each strike a drawing of the sword, a killing blow, then back into its sheathe. But the martial form was not the true strength of Rage of Lightning. The true power was in the linked techniques.

Daijiro yelled in alarm as a paw swipe cracked the stone at his feet. He was stabbing retreating, stabbing retreating, each step a hair from being savaged by the shishi.

Ichiro pulled on the atmosphere around him and lightning

shot upwards from the clouds, six different bolts streaking into the air, arcing around and merging on him, forming into a crackling cage of electricity.

"Get out of the way, Daijiro," Ichiro shouted. He couldn't hold the lightning long, or it would use him as a conduit to the ground.

Daijiro glanced at him, startled, then threw himself to the floor. The shishi pounced.

"Dragon's Breath!" Ichiro shouted and drew his dagger into a thrusting stab. The lightning flowed through the blade and formed into a roaring dragon's head written in flashing blue lines. It streaked through the air and slammed into the shishi with a crack louder than thunder. The statue burst apart and fell into six smoking pieces.

Ichiro blew out a breath and let go of the energy and the sword form. He hadn't expected that to work.

Daijiro scrambled to his feet, and backed away from the smoking rubble. "Cutting it close there, Aniki."

Ichiro joined his brother. "Gotta make it dramatic, you know. That other one isn't going to come alive is it? Because I don't think I have another one of those in me."

Daijiro shook his head. "Mouth open on that one."

"Aaand?"

"It represents life, not death. How do you not know that? You really should read a book sometime."

They started towards the temple, where the donkey was still cowering, dark eyes wide with terror. "Thanks for that. I didn't think you'd mastered lightning," Daijiro said.

Ichiro shrugged. "I've been practicing."

"Good for you. And for me apparently. You know all six forms now then?"

"Nah. Still missing the last one."

"Not practicing that hard, then?"

Ichiro glared at him. “I’ll remember you said that next time you need saving from a living statue.”

They collected the donkey with only a few calming words needed and stepped up before the temple. “You don't think there's any more surprises waiting for us up there?” Daijiro asked.

Ichiro shook his head. Now they were so close, with nothing left in their way, he felt apprehensive.

“Alright then!” Daijiro took a deep breath and blew out an explosive sigh. “Let's do this.”

THE SWORD IN THE ASHES

With the end in sight.
One final test to see through.
The final farewell.

Ichiro was expecting a grand temple to the gods when he pulled open the door. Instead, he found a bare room, large and undecorated, as though whoever built it had poured all their time into the impressive facade outside and had neglected the interior. There was a staircase in the middle of the room, leading upwards, and the far wall was dominated by an open window facing the sky and clouds. In front of that window stood a young boy wearing black funeral robes, and a bright red scarf around his neck. The boy was barefoot, staring out at the stars. He did not turn to them when they entered.

Daijiro stepped forward, opening his mouth to speak, but Ichiro grabbed his arm and hauled him back, giving him a sharp shake of his head. The shinigami were the most dangerous of all spirits. It was their job to ferry the dead from realm to realm, and most people well knew that not even the gods could completely control the reapers. It was said the shinigami wore many guises, but they were forever cursed to walk barefoot to feel the consequences of their actions.

The young boy did not turn from his silent vigil, but Ichiro bowed low anyway, pulling Daijiro down with him, then they hurried up the stairs, dragging the donkey with them. It was never wise to come to the attention of a reaper.

"Do I want to know?" Daijiro asked once they were out of sight. Ichiro just shook his head. He didn't even want to think about the near encounter.

The temple roof was stone and open to the stars above, and night was gathering about them. A pyre was already set up, a crosshatch of logs soaked in oil.

"That's a bit odd, isn't it?" Daijiro asked. "Almost like they knew we were coming. They… They. Whoever they is. What? It's just odd." He was babbling.

"Of all the things we've seen on our way up here, this is the bit that strikes you as odd?"

Daijiro huffed. "The rest of it was weird. This is odd."

"You were swallowed by a toad."

"Which was very weird."

Ichiro thumped his brother on the arm and smiled. They set about unlashing Subaru's corpse from the donkey, and Ichiro half expected the beast to bolt the moment it was free, but the smelly creature just sat and watched as they carried Subaru and set him down on the pyre. Perhaps, after carrying the burden all this way, it, too wanted to see the funeral through.

They were ready.

"Someone should say something, don't you think?" Daijiro said. He was always even more chatty than normal when anxious. "Do you want to say something? You were the oldest."

Ichiro shook his head. He was struggling to make sense of the tightness in his chest, the fuzzy edges of his sight.

Daijiro reached into his furs and pulled out a small clay flask. He pulled the cork free and swigged deep, then handed it to Ichiro.

Daijiro cleared his throat, then said, "To Subaru. What an arsehole!"

Ichiro swigged at the flask, not even tasting the alcohol, then stepped forward and placed the flask on the pyre next to Subaru. The last drink the Brothers Blood would ever share as three.

"You were the best brother I could have hoped for," Daijiro continued, his voice tight. "And the worst. Never met a fight you didn't want, nor a tail you couldn't chase. And you always had my back, brother. Until you didn't, I guess, but... Ahh, fuck it. I miss you, little brother."

Daijiro wiped his eyes and nudged Ichiro. "Sure you don't want to say anything?"

Ichiro shook his head.

"Fair enough. Do the honours, then."

Ichiro drew the little knife and had to force the words through a constricting throat. "Six Element Style: Hunger of Flames. Burning Brand." The knife glowed orange, then red, and burst into flames. Ichiro advanced on the pyre and bent to light it.

He stopped, eyes blurry from tears. He couldn't do it.

Ichiro took a step back and let the knife fall from limp fingers. The flames guttered out.

"Aniki?" Daijiro said.

Ichiro turned to his last living brother and felt hot tears stinging his eyes. "I'm not ready. I can't... He's not allowed to be dead."

"I know."

Ichiro shook his head. "No. It's not right. I know it's not right, but I'm angry at him. How is it I'm furious at Subaru for dying? How dare he leave us? It's not fair that he died before he told me who he really was. Before I had the chance to accept it. It's not fair that he's dead, and we're not, and now we have to go on without him. And I am so angry at him for it."

Ichiro sagged and Daijiro rushed forward, wrapped him in an embrace. "And I just want... I want him to come back. I just want Subaru to come strolling up those steps, and this whole thing to be another one of his stupid pranks."

They both glanced at the steps, hoping it would be true. But there was no Subaru, only the donkey.

"But he won't come back. Because he's gone. He's gone and I miss him, Daijiro. I missed both of you for years, and now he's gone, I don't get to take any of that time back. It's gone. He's gone."

"He's not gone, brother," Daijiro said in a shaky voice. "Not really. He'll always be there in our memories. But more than that, he's here in us. In who we are. Neither of us would be who we are today, without him. His stupid jokes, his overconfidence, his damned pride, they all helped shape us both. As much as we helped shape him. So whatever we do, he's here with us. Always will be. As long as one of the Brothers Blood stands, we all stand with him. Yeah?"

Ichiro took a great, shaky breath. "Yeah."

"But he's still an arsehole for dying."

Ichiro chuckled through the tears and bent to pick up the knife. "Burning..." The words died in his constricting throat, and he sobbed again.

"What would Subaru say?" Daijiro asked.

"Stop being a wet eel, and send me to heaven, you prick," Ichiro said with a sobbing laugh. Then he sobered and it was almost as if Subaru was with them, as if he could hear his little brother speaking the words along with him.

"He'd say I love you. Both of you. And no matter what happened between us, and where our lives took us, we were and always will be brothers. Beyond blood. Now send me to heaven, you prick."

Ichiro lit the pyre. The flames tore through the wood hungrily and then found the body atop it, and Blood Subaru burned.

Ichiro backed up and knelt before the flames. Daijiro sat next to him, and they kept vigil as they sent their little brother off.

The logs cracked and a puff of bright embers plumed up into the sky to mix with the stars. Behind them, the donkey gave a startled bray. The beast had wide eyes, staring around like it had no idea where it was. Then it leapt up and bolted down the steps.

"Wait." Daijiro scratched at his chin. "You said the spirits of the dead can possess animals. You don't think..."

Ichiro laughed and nodded. Subaru's one last prank. He had been with them all along.

"If the stories are true, and each star is one of our ancestors watching over us, which one is Subaru?" Ichiro said.

Daijiro stared at the sky for a few minutes, then pointed. "See that constellation?" He traced the outline with his finger. "Looks like a giant cock, and that's Subaru right at the head."

Ichiro laughed and nodded. "Perfect."

Daijiro pulled another flask from his furs, and they shared a drink, keeping watch until morning, until all the embers had died and there was nothing left of their brother but ash and memories.

"Now what?" Daijiro asked as the sun broke through the clouds, chasing away the night and Subaru's new star.

Ichiro wiped at grimy eyes. "Now we go back to our lives, brother. You have your monks to train, I have my students to teach. I understand what Subaru started now, but we're not him. We can't do what he did."

Daijiro grunted, nodding in agreement. "I know, Aniki. I know. I just thought maybe we should pay tribute to Subaru. One last time, yeah?"

Ichiro chuckled. "What was all this if not paying him a final tribute?"

"Yeah, I know. Just..." Daijiro let out a pointed sigh. Ichiro knew how he felt, he wasn't ready to say goodbye yet either. Who knew when they'd see each other again.

He closed his eyes and let the peace of the mountaintop flow through him. "What did you have in mind?"

"Well..." Daijiro said, clapping his hands. "We have to pass back through Ringen, right? A whole town full of folk being oppressed by bandits who don't know the proper spirit of the job. I reckon Subaru would want that dealt with!"

Ichiro scoffed. "You want us to fight a whole town full of bandits? Daijiro, I don't even have a sword."

Daijiro nudged him and cleared his throat. Then again. more insistently.

"What?" Ichiro asked, opening his eyes.

Daijiro pointed to the still smoking pyre. There, lying amongst the ashes was a shining glint of steel. A katana resting within his brother's ashen remains.

Ichiro didn't know if Subaru had planned it all along somehow, or if it was a last gift from his brother now he was in heaven. He supposed the how of it didn't matter. He shook his head and couldn't stop the smile from splitting his lips.

"Arsehole!"

AFTERWORD

Thank you for reading Blood Brothers Beyond. I'd like to take this opportunity to tell a little tale about where this story came from.

A few years ago, I lost a brother. It was sudden. Peaceful, but very unexpected. And for a while, it broke me. I simply did not know how to deal with him no longer being there. I kept expecting to get a message from him, or seeing memes and knowing if I sent them to him he'd get a good laugh. For a long time it just didn't feel real.

And to be honest, the loss is something I'm still dealing with.

Enter the Brothers Blood. Earlier this year, this story popped into my head and I felt it was something I needed to write as a way to explore my own grief. Now I'm not saying I'm Ichiro, and as far as I know my brother was not a cross-dressing crime lord, but in writing these characters and this story, I managed to put into words some of the emotions that have been rattling around inside my head and heart for a long time. This is a story about exploring grief and loss, and it also just so happens that the Mortal Techniques world has the exploration of trauma at its core.

So once again, thank you for reading.

And if you did enjoy it, please do consider leaving the book a rating or review on Amazon or Goodreads or any other reviewing platform. Reviews are incredibly useful for authors to help recommend our books so I would be eternally grateful.

If you would like to continue your journey through the world of the Mortal Techniques, I have a short story (*The Two Faces of War*) set in the world available for **FREE** through my newsletter. Don't worry, I won't spam your inbox, but by signing up you'll be notified of all my new releases, have a chance at winning monthly loot giveaways, and get access to **three** exclusive short stories.

You can sign up for my newsletter on my website (www.robjhayes.co.uk) or by following this link.

Again, thank you for reading!

ROB

BOOKS BY ROB J. HAYES

The God Eater Saga (Heroic Epic Fantasy)

Herald (Age of the God Eater #1)

Deathless (Annals of the God Eater #1)

Demon (Archive of the God Eater #1)

The War Eternal (Dark Epic Fantasy)

Along the Razor's Edge

The Lessons Never Learned

From Cold Ashes Risen

Sins of the Mother

Death's Beating Heart

Titan Hoppers (Coming of Age Sci-Fantasy)

Titan Hoppers

Spire Climbers

Fleet Champions

The Mortal Techniques (Asian Sword & Sorcery)

Never Die

Pawn's Gambit

Spirits of Vengeance

The Century Blade (short story)

Beyond Brothers Blood (novella)

The First Earth Saga (Grimdark Fantasy)

The Heresy Within (The Ties that Bind #1)

The Colour of Vengeance (The Ties that Bind #2)

The Price of Faith (The Ties that Bind #3)

Where Loyalties Lie (Best Laid Plans #1)

The Fifth Empire of Man (Best Laid Plans #2)

City of Kings

It Takes a Thief... (Lighthearted Steampunk)

It Takes a Thief to Catch a Sunrise

It Takes a Thief to Start a Fire

www.ingramcontent.com/pod-product-compliance
Lightning Source LLC
Chambersburg PA
CBHW020503310726
48979CB00016B/2767/J

* 9 7 8 1 9 1 5 4 4 0 0 9 9 *